THERE IS NO OTHER

THERE IS
NO OTHER

Jonathan Papernick

Exile Editions

Publishers of singular
Fiction, Poetry, Translation, Drama, and Nonfiction

2010

Library and Archives Canada Cataloguing in Publication

Papernick, Jon
    There is no other / Jonathan Papernick.

Short stories.
ISBN 978-1-55096-138-6

    I. Title.

PS8581.A6645T54 2010   C813'.6   C2010-900790-5

Cover Paper Design by Ed Blitzkrieg
Text and Cover Design and Composition by Digital ReproSet
Typeset in Minion fonts at the Moons of Jupiter Studios
Printed in Canada by Imprimerie Gauvin

The publisher would like to acknowledge the financial assistance of
the Canada Council for the Arts and the Ontario Arts Council, which is
an agency of the Government of Ontario.

Conseil des Arts du Canada   Canada Council for the Arts

ONTARIO ARTS COUNCIL
CONSEIL DES ARTS DE L'ONTARIO

Published in Canada in 2010 by Exile Editions Ltd.
144483 Southgate Road 14 – Gen Del
Holstein, Ontario, N0G 2A0
info@exileeditions.com
www.ExileEditions.com

Canadian Sales Distribution:
McArthur & Company, c/o Harper Collins, 1995 Markham Road
Toronto, ON, M1B 5M8 ~ toll free: 1 800 387 0117

U.S. Sales Distribution:
Independent Publishers Group, 814 North Franklin Street, Chicago, IL, 60610
www.ipgbook.com ~ toll free: 1 800 888 4741

For Zev and Jesse
My Two Miracles

Also by Jonathan Papernick

THE ASCENT OF ELI ISRAEL
WHO BY FIRE, WHO BY BLOOD

Contents

~

Skin for Skin

Her parents were four hours up the Interstate celebrating her baby cousin's *bris* in Albany, and the new boy from English class, who quoted Nietzsche to the impertinent Miss Meade, sat shirtless on the orange rec room couch. Breath laced with cooking sherry and Marlboros, he was irresistible. His pale, concave chest scored with angry red pimples spoke of punk rock and wild abandon; his lithe body, a knife ready to spring. They made out in the darkness, side one of *Astral Weeks* spinning on the turntable. He pressed closer and touched her cheek tenderly, the throbbing vein in her neck, the gently curved clavicle she broke in a fall from her first bicycle. He wasn't a spastic mauler like the rest of the mediocrities at her high school, not a clueless virgin impersonating the porn stars the other boys watched on their parents' VCRs.

She whispered his name, halting his progression.

His voice was entirely changed. "You want to do it?"

He took his time flipping the hair from his eyes in a gesture meant to seem casual, and removed his wallet from his jeans' pocket, lightly fingering the raised circular impression to assure her that he had come prepared.

She felt the cool bite of his necklace against her skin, the pendant swinging around back as her fingers blindly explored his body, and she imagined a tiny motorcycle or pistol, something fearless strung at the end of the chain. And now, as he reset the pendant to its proper position dangling at his solar plexus, she realized that the constriction in her throat was entirely involuntary, and that the delirious moments before its appearance marked the end of a lifelong dream. Even in the basement's gloom she could see it clearly, iridescent, glowing dangerously between them, like something aflame.

"Take it off," she said, reaching for the gold crucifix at his neck. It was heavy; the miniature corpse reproduced in minute detail weighed something like two thousand years in her trembling hands.

"Why? Are you Jewish?"

"My parents are."

"That's cool." He laughed and dipped in for another kiss, but she wasn't having it.

She told him to take it off or forget the whole thing. He hesitated, not sure she was serious, then fumbled with the crucifix before lifting it over his head with great difficulty, as if he were bearing the True Cross on his narrow shoulders, then tossed it across the floor.

"Now what are you going to take off?"

"I'm done," she said.

He tucked a loose strand of hair behind her ear. "What's your problem?"

He told her he had come all this way by bus and she owed him something. She knew what happened to girls who went back on the unspoken contract that was made when they invited boys over with their parents out of town. She had always thought a cocktease was worse than a whore, and now she faced the sickening prospect that everyone in her school would know what she was.

She had been with non-Jewish boys before, one or two had even worn simple crosses, but nobody so bold as to parade a gory crucifix before her eyes.

She had naturally turned away from being part of an unlucky, persecuted tribe. The way she saw it, there was no gain in membership, only grief. "I'm not Jewish," she had told her parents hundreds of times. "I'm a secular humanist and I believe in self-determination." She thought ritual circumcision was barbaric. But now, as he slid his hand around her waist, she wished that she were with her parents and aunts and uncles celebrating her eight-day-old cousin's covenant with God and the Jewish people. That was where she belonged, not here in a darkened basement with a nasty, crude boy determined to have his way.

He stood naked before her, wearing only a pair of white gym socks that smelled like they hadn't been washed in a very long time. "Your turn," he said.

Now in the dim light she saw it clearly against his livid thigh and it shocked her more than the appearance of the crucifix, like the emergence of a sea monster from a bathtub.

"No. I can't." She had never seen anything like it before, but had heard somewhere that uncircumcised men were likely to give their partners greater pleasure. She could not believe that.

He didn't seem fazed by her reaction at all, as if *no* were simply a prelude.

"Come on. It's getting late." And then, "I can ruin you."

She thought of all the combinations of what might happen if he shot his mouth off around school, and she determined that she would be better off doing it with him to avoid a public shaming.

There was just one small thing.

"I'll be right back," she said, climbing off the couch and heading for the stairs.

She returned a few minutes later with a sharp Japanese paring knife that her mother used for salads in the summer, a bag of cotton balls and a bottle of witch hazel. "Okay, I'll do it," she said. "But first you have to let me fix something."

There Is No Other

Jenny Kagan, dressed in her shimmering Wonder Woman outfit, was already waiting outside the classroom door when Aaron Needle arrived at 7:15 a.m. to prepare for the coming school day. Needle, dressed in his customary checked blazer and slacks, a small frayed-at-the-edges knit *kippa* covering most of the bald patch on the top of his head, could barely mutter, "Good morning." He wished he had downed his first coffee on the train in from Midwood, but he had inadvertently dumped it on the subway platform when someone had asked him the time. His sacred sense of mission rarely kicked in before his third cup, and now he found himself staring bleary-eyed into the face of one of his charges.

"Is it really a good morning, Mr. Needle?" She smiled as she tossed a silken yellow cord over his narrow shoulder. "This is the Lasso of Truth made from the Goddess Gaia's golden girdle."

"Alliteration. Clever," he said, sliding out from under the lasso. "Isn't it a bit early?"

"My mother has a breakfast meeting. In the city," she said, rolling her eyes. She jammed a wilted cardboard box into his hands. "*Hamantashens.*"

Next to arrive was Avi Dorfman, the only six-and-a-half-foot-tall seventh grader Needle had seen in all his years of teaching, dressed as a wan, stoop-shouldered Derek Jeter. Sarah Sherman was dressed as Amelia Earhart, Max Rosenbaum as Nosferatu, and four-eyed Max Carp as a FDNY captain. By 8:30, the room was crowded with miniature facsimiles of Jedi Knights clashing lightsabers by the craft closet, a Harry Potter, a cross-dressing Hermione and Lord Voldemort himself. More disturbingly, there were two Britney Spears in blond wigs and suggestive outfits, and one less than virginal-looking Madonna. As he scanned the room, Needle saw not one single Queen Esther, or Mordecai, or even King Achash-verosh, and he shook his head sadly. These were his children, after all.

The year of Needle's Bar Mitzvah, his neighbor Morton Gass had been publicly scolded by their teacher for doing his part to destroy Jewish heritage simply because he came to school dressed as the great Sandy Koufax.

It happened so subtly that it had almost escaped Needle's notice. The festival of Purim had slowly morphed into little more than an empty pageant, a Jewish Halloween. Nonetheless, Needle was surprised every year.

He noticed Dorfman's Derek Jeter trade a crudely autographed baseball with Leslie Maslow's Madonna in exchange for a kabbalistic red string that was supposed to ward off bad luck and the evil eye. He stared in amazement for a moment, because Dorfman, seemingly emboldened by his chosen alter ego, was speaking to a girl for the first time since he had slumped into class last September.

Needle believed the aphorism: The world itself rests upon the breath of the children in the schoolhouse. And he saw this as a teaching opportunity.

"I know you're all excited about the celebration of the Book of Esther," Needle said. "But let's quieten down a moment."

After the students had taken their seats, Needle gestured to a red-faced Avi Dorfman, who was having difficulty tying the string around his thin wrist.

"Where did you get that string, Mr. Dorfman?"

"Um," he replied.

"And Ms. Maslow, I see that you possess an autographed baseball. I trust that you're not going to eat it."

"No," she barely whispered, covering her silver braces with the palm of her hand.

"Who can tell me the meaning of *mishloach manot*?" He let the question hang in the air for a full two minutes of sadistic silence. There had been a time when every Jew that he knew engaged in the practice of sending gifts, food mostly, to family, friends and neighbors to celebrate the holiday of Purim.

"Jenny?" Needle said after a moment, pointing to Wonder Woman shrinking in the first row. "You brought *hamantashen* today. Please tell me that you know why."

He held one up before the class.

Needle heard a sudden shock of laughter, and instinctively checked to see if his fly was down.

How, when he had mentally taken attendance as his students arrived that morning, could he have forgotten Junius Barker? It was wishful thinking, for sure. But Junius had missed the previous week's classes without a word of explanation, and Needle had found a way to push him from his mind, the way he had, during his lonely teenage years, managed to forget his father's *yahrzeit.* Now, that raspy, cocksure voice, the biggest pain in his ass since he'd been hired to teach at the Downtown Jewish Day School, was calling him a bloodsucking infidel.

Junius always had something to say with that mouth of his, whether he was questioning the brutality of ritual circumcision and promising to show the class how he had been scarred for life, or wondering why the Jews had a claim to land in Palestine when it was Europeans who had evicted them *en masse* from their homes and slaughtered them for the sport of it.

He must have ridden all the way from Neptune Avenue completely beneath the notice of the blinkered commuters rushing off to work in the city, their eyes focused on the gray rain slashing against the train's tempered windows. Because, when Needle turned around, he saw something he hoped he would never see in his class: the brown-skinned Junius Barker, all five feet of him, draped in a flowing white robe, a turban wound around his head, a rough beard pasted to his cherubic cheeks, and a bandolier of what might have been dynamite strapped in the form of an X across his gamecock chest.

"*Allahu Akbar*! God is the greatest!" Junius shouted, and slammed the classroom door shut behind him, locking it.

The kids in the class often joked that he had been sent to the Downtown Jewish Day School to put the Jew back in Junius, and whispered that his arrival followed a year spent in juvie. But Needle knew that Junius had been homeschooled the previous year, and that his father, a Haitian immigrant who taught engineering at Polytechnic University, and mother, the sole offspring of Polish Holocaust survivors, had, despite Junius' IQ of 160, been frustrated by the heads of enrollment at more than a dozen private schools in Brooklyn and Manhattan because of Junius' wild reputation at PS 100. The DJDS, however, ascribed to a strained amalgam of squishy Liberalism and Jewish renewal, and pretty much accepted anyone who claimed to be Jewish. When the curly-haired black boy had been brought to Needle the week before classes began, he was reminded of the school's motto that a child is not an empty vessel, but a flame to be kindled, and he knew that he could light a fire under this child. But that was September and since then, six long months had passed.

"Junius. You're late. Please take your seat."

"I am the prophet Mohammed, cocksucker," Junius responded. "I will not sit at the back of the class like some second-rate prophet. I am the messenger of God."

The students laughed as the diminutive prophet began chanting a mixture of pidgin Arabic gleaned from the evening news and assorted multi-syllabic vulgarities. Needle drew a long breath, searching deep inside for the strength to face this latest challenge. The last time he had confronted Junius, he had been called an unreconstructed racist by the child, and Ms. Schulhof, the headmistress, had suggested that he be more sensitive with the school's minorities, a short roster which included three adopted Asians, named Moses, Joshua and Rebecca, as well as a half-dozen or so biracial children. The school psychologist advised that Junius was not sufficiently challenged in the classroom, but Needle thought this just another New Age excuse for laziness and bad behavior.

"All right, all right," Needle said. "Come on in and take a seat. But you need to change that outfit before the Megillah reading."

"Outfit?" Junius said. "This is no outfit."

"Mr. Needle," Dorfman called, "can I please go to the bathroom?" His voice seemed to be changing mid-sentence.

"Not now," Needle said. He turned his attention back to Junius. "I trust that is not dynamite."

"You mean dy-no-mite!" Junius said, imitating an old sitcom that he must have seen on Nickelodeon.

"It's just freakin' fireworks," Max Rosenbaum interjected, laughing his horsy laugh. "My parents took me to Graceland last summer. They sell them in supermarkets all over the South. It's just fireworks. Obviously."

"Junius, you know that I appreciate your creativity and originality, but I'm going to have to ask you to leave unless you take off that outfit right now. This is an old building and fireworks are forbidden."

"Have it your way," he said, dropping his robe to the ground.

Leslie Maslow cried out, "Oh my God," and Avi Dorfman broke into tears and called for his mother. Some of the kids had grown up in the shadows of the World Trade Center, and they sobbed quietly at their desks.

Beneath the robe, Junius wore a camouflage vest. His pockets were stuffed with white bricks of something that looked like clay. But what concerned Needle and the rest of the suddenly terrified class were the wires that ran into a small black detonator that the smiling Junius held in his hand. He unwrapped the bandolier from his chest and gestured to the bricks in his vest. "This is military-grade C-4 explosive. Got it on the Internet. And it's going to take some of us to heaven. Hey, Jedi," he called. "Are you supposed to be Luke or Anakin Skywalker?"

The student answered that he was Anakin, the future Darth Vader.

"Perfect. Help me string this up."

The frightened child looked wide-eyed at Needle for instruction, but misread his signal to stay seated and instead bounded up to the front of the class to begin pinning the strings of dynamite to the cork boards beneath the colorful time chart of Jewish history.

Ever since the shootings at Columbine, Needle had been mentally preparing to deal with his own massacre, though he had imagined a drugged-out homeboy stumbling in from the Fulton Mall with a stolen nine millimeter in search of God-knows-what in the science lab. Needle's crisis training had taught him to ask the little maniac what he wanted.

"That's for me to know and you to find out." Junius smiled and tapped on the side of the detonator. "And call me Mohammed or don't call me at all."

"All right, Mohammed," Needle said, his voice full of fatigue. "What can I do for you?"

"What can you *Jew* for me?" Junius laughed. "How about telling me why Jews eat Haman's ear at Purim," he said, enunciating the more graphic Hebrew term for *hamantashen*, "and not Hitler's unkosher sauerkraut cock the rest of the year?"

"I think you just answered that question for yourself."

"But Hitler and Haman both tried to kill the Jews. There's no food to celebrate the Holocaust."

"All right, all right, Junius. You've tweaked the nose of everyone in this class, now why don't you take a seat—"

"It's Mohammed, goddammit."

Needle suddenly remembered that he was talking with a seventh grader whose gaps in knowledge were as wide as the East River. He had to reassert himself the only way he knew how. "Can you tell me the Five Pillars of Islam?"

"You think I don't know them?" Junius said, full of his trademark swagger.

"You do know that it's against Islam to portray the Prophet? You do know that?" Needle pressed. "Do you think there are seventy-two virgins waiting for you in heaven?"

"I don't know," Junius said. "You're supposed to be the teacher. You tell me what's waiting up in heaven."

Needle had thought often of the world to come, especially during his long train rides to and from work; he wondered whether his parents were waiting on the other side to shower him, at long last, with hugs and kisses.

"Family, friends, people from history."

"Like a big cocktail party?" Junius teased.

"No," Needle said.

"Then what?"

"I don't know."

"Clouds and harps and angels?"

"Don't be ridiculous."

"You're the one who thinks you're going to see your parents' cancer-ridden bodies doing the tango up there in the stars, with Moses on the left and Buddha on the right."

"Stop mocking, Junius."

"I'm not mocking Junius, I'm mocking you. Now tell me, what is it like on the other side?"

"I don't know," Needle expelled after a long pause.

"You think you're pretty smart, Needle. You know, those who can't do, teach. Well, what about those who can't teach? Whatever. Now I'm calling the shots." He waved the detonator before the class.

"Mr. Needle, I've got to pee," Dorfman cried.

"So, you're not a Jew anymore, Junius. Is that it? Please tell me that you're not going to hurt these children simply because they are Jewish and you are frustrated with the complexities of Judaism. Tell me it's not so. Didn't you say your grandmother survived the *Shoah*?"

"Don't persecute me because of her weakness," Junius said. "For your information, she was in a brothel in Berlin." He began pacing towards the first row of seats.

"Let's just put the detonator down before someone gets hurt."

"Nope," Junius said, shaking his head.

Needle wished that he could fatten himself out and become a wall of kryptonite separating Junius from the rest of the class. Surely Needle would sacrifice his life to save those of the twenty-one innocent kids under his care. He had no children of his own, and saving the lives of these students would carry his name on through the collective eternity of their memories. But Needle knew that this was impossible and he was suddenly afraid that one of his students, emboldened by a designer costume, would try to play superhero and grab for the explosives as Junius passed; they were seventh graders after all, and prone to flights of imagination.

The class sat stiff and frightened, as Junius strutted up one row and down the next, shouting at his classmates as he went: "For your information, Sophia, I don't celebrate Kwanzaa, I don't live in the ghetto, I don't listen to gangsta rap. And by the way, isn't your mother a convert?" He tapped Sam Michaels, a sunken Harry Potter, on the shoulder of his cape, "And you, *putz*, Yiddish is not just a Jewish version of Pig Latin."

"I was joking," Michaels whimpered.

"And Ezra, you pathetic Eminem wannabe, your father's supposed to be a rabbi. Wasn't he just accused of stealing money from the synagogue to support his mistress?"

Junius pointed generally towards the back of the class. "And the *kiddush* is not the same as the *Kaddish*. Don't you Jews know anything at all? It's the prayer they say for you after you die," he taunted, waving the detonator.

The classroom smelled damp and sheepy from all the rain-soaked coats and capes and wigs, and Needle was fleetingly reminded of his own childhood and the cold winters before his parents had died, his father dressing early in the morning to say *Kaddish* for his own father at the local synagogue. Now Needle was older than his father had been when he died, and Needle felt that he had reached extra innings. He wondered briefly who would say *Kaddish* for him when he was gone.

"It's the prayer they say after you die," Junius repeated.

Several of the students' eyes pooled with tears, and Dorfman cried out, "I don't want to die."

"We're all going to die," Junius said.

"Junius, just take a deep breath," Needle said. "Relax. Nobody here is going to die."

Max Rosenbaum sat tilted back in his chair, wearing a foolish bucktoothed smile on his face. "Dorfman peed," he offered, pointing to the gawky child in the Yankees uniform, whose head was buried in his arms on his desk.

Dorfman had indeed peed in his pinstripes, and the urine was forming a puddle at his feet.

Junius stood at the front of the class squeaking the words CHOSEN PEOPLE onto the whiteboard with a thick marker.

"Whatever happened to the blackboard?" Junius laughed. "White is right, I guess."

"Junius," Needle said. "Avi needs to go to the bathroom. Will you let him go?"

"I think it's too late," Junius laughed. "But, I *will* let your people go, if they can answer some questions for me." His voice dripped with contempt.

Needle advanced a step towards Junius, his shoulders back, spine straightened to exert authority. "Stop this right now," he whispered between gritted teeth. "Before you get yourself into serious trouble."

But Junius, his voice thick with righteousness, shouted, "Don't move or I'll blow this place up, motherfucker. Now, can someone tell me why in the world the Jews are the Chosen People?" He knuckled the large block letters he'd written on the board. "And you, Needle, zip it. You have all the answers, don't you? Does somebody want to tell me why the Jews are the Chosen People?"

There was some chattering from the back of the class and Needle saw someone's hand shoot up. It was Suzi Grossman, one of the two Britney Spears. "If I answer this," she said, "you'll let me go, right?"

Junius nodded his head and seemed to be pleased by the power that he wielded over his classmates.

"The – Jews – are – the – Chosen – People – because – God – favored – them – over – all – others," she said slowly and deliberately, as if trying to remember a specific statement she had once heard.

Junius made a buzzing sound announcing that she was wrong. "I thought you were going to say that it was because you're getting a Bloomingdale's credit card for your Bat Mitzvah. Anyone else?"

Max Carp, the former sixth-grade national chess champion, answered that the Jews were simply smarter than all other people, with more doctors and lawyers and writers *per capita* and so on; therefore, it was natural that they were the Chosen People.

"Chosen for what?" Junius pressed. "To chase ambulances? Perform nose jobs?"

This was a question that Needle had been asking himself all his life. He knew the answer, of course: Jews had been chosen to enter into a covenant with God and to follow His laws. But philosophically, Needle felt that the Jews had been chosen to suffer. It was true throughout history and no different in his case. He had been orphaned as a child and brought up by a distant aunt. Needle had never really connected with anyone, male or female. He knew every kind of loneliness and lived alone in a one-bedroom apartment in the back of his land- lord's house off Ocean Parkway. Waiting. Waiting for what? Perhaps this was the day he had been waiting for his entire life, an end to it all, an express elevator ride to the Gates of Heaven.

"The Muslims say there is one God, and the Christians say there is one God, except the Catholics who have the Father, the Son and the Holy Ghost, and the Jews say there is one God. Which one is the true God and how come they are all so fucking hard to find? And if all these believers are in with one true God, why are the Jews the Chosen People?"

"Junius, we received the Torah at Mount Sinai."

"And who told you that, Needle? Charlton fucking Heston?"

"My father told me, and his father told him and so on, all the way back through time."

"I can't imagine why somebody might lie about such a thing. A bit self-serving for a disempowered, perse- cuted people. It's masterful propaganda," Junius said.

"You don't know what you're talking about," Needle said. "You smash anything in your way just so you can see it break."

"I'll choose 'iconoclast' for one thousand dollars."

"You're speaking from complete ignorance, Junius. You think you're a rebel, but really you're just a lazy, sheltered child with no understanding of the scope of history, and the power of prayer to keep a people going through hard times."

"Boo-yah," Junius pointed at Needle with his extended index finger.

Now Needle saw that Junius was mumbling a familiar prayer, a prayer that Needle had repeated by rote his entire life so that it had almost lost all meaning. Junius' voice rose above the murmuring of the other students, eyes rolled back in his head, and Needle realized that this child, turbaned and strapped with explosives, was singing the *Aleinu* in a voice that soared beneath the humming fluorescent lights like a beautiful rare bird. The boy's body swayed limply as if he had been emptied out to fuel that voice. Needle had never heard anything like it, and he joined with Junius, singing the final lines, which in English mean: "You shall know today, and take to heart, that *Adonai* is the only God, in the heavens above and on earth below. There is no other."

The class sat in stunned silence. Needle was certain that not a single child in his class could recall all the lines of the *Aleinu*, not to mention sing it with such otherworldly precision. "Nicely done, Junius. That was remarkable," Needle said.

The boy looked winded, confused, as if he had just returned from a long journey through the celestial heights and did not know where he had landed. He wobbled back and forth as if he might fall over and then the flame returned to his eyes.

"Junius, are you all right?" Needle asked.

"Yeah," he said in a faraway tone.

"Take off that ridiculous costume. You are no more Mohammed than I am Elvis."

"It's Purim," Junius said, his voice soft and vulnerable. "I just wanted to know what it felt like to be Haman."

"And how does that feel?"

"Not as good as I thought it would."

"I understand. You were trying to reenact the story of Purim for the class," Needle said, his stomach fluttering with a strange feeling of satisfaction that might have been joy. His words over the past six months, had, in fact, penetrated Junius' skull. "Now, why don't you take off that silly beard and join the rest of the class for the Megillah reading?" He removed his watch from his jacket pocket. "We're late."

Junius, chastened somewhat by Needle's appeasing tone, peeled the beard back from his face. His cheeks, round and shining like burnished apples, were still padded with the final remnants of baby fat.

A voice over the intercom, harsh and piercing, announced, "Will Mr. Needle's class please proceed to the cafetorium for the Purim *shpiel*. We are all waiting for you." The voice was loud, flat and toneless with a Bronx accent, and felt to Needle like a hammer blow to his head.

This was the voice that regularly called Junius to the front office for detention, and he slammed his hand against the whiteboard and said, "We're not leaving here until someone can tell me why I am less of a Jew because I am black."

Needle heard titters from the back of the class.

"My mom is Jewish," Junius cried. "Does that mean that I am only half a chosen person because my dad swam here from some shitty little island?"

More laughter.

But Junius was not joking. "Stop laughing because there is enough C-4 to wipe those smiles off your faces forever."

"Junius," Needle said.

"Don't take one step closer," he warned, his shaking finger on the detonator. "I'm serious."

"You don't want to do this."

"I want to know which half of me is chosen, the top half or the bottom, the inside or the outside, or the other way around? Why is it so hard to figure out? If God separated Jews from the other nations and gave them a different destiny, which half of me is chosen, which half of me bows down before the King of Kings, and which half can go fuck himself?"

"Junius," Needle said. "Sometimes we choose to be chosen, and you, you have chosen."

"I didn't choose this life."

"Junius, we can talk about this later on, but right now I need you to—"

Ms. Schulhof's voice was outside the door. "Mr. Needle, open this door right now. Locking doors is not the DJDS way."

"Why is it so hard for me to be a Jew, when you all can skip temple on Yom Kippur, take off for your country houses and no one doubts that you are Jewish, but when I go to synagogue people are always asking what I am doing there? Do they think I'm going to steal their precious *tallitot*? I have to work twice as hard as the rest of you and I still don't belong." Now his voice cracked. "My *bubbe* spent two years in Auschwitz, and she died last week of a fucking cold. She always called me her little *pitzel*. She never once called me nigger."

There was an insistent knocking at the door, and Ms. Schulhof's voice rose like an alien sound above the banging.

"Tell her to back off, Needle. Tell her to step back and nobody will get hurt." Junius waved the detonator in the air like he was holding aloft an adversary's scalp.

Needle responded in a voice that he did not recognize, firm and forceful, telling Ms. Schulhof he needed five more minutes. "Junius," Needle said, "I'm so sorry to hear about your *bubbe*. What can I do for you? What do you need?"

The banging continued outside the door, and Needle could see the brass knob jiggling. But these were strong steel fire doors that had been installed just five years earlier when the DJDS had taken possession of the old building. Some students were hiding behind their overturned desks now, costumes trailing out into the empty aisles. A couple of the students had folded themselves into the craft closet at the back of the classroom and managed to close the door behind them.

"Do you believe in God?" Junius asked.

"Of course," Needle answered.

"Say it," Junius said.

"I believe in God."

"Which one? The one that gives, or the one that takes away?"

Needle heard sirens blaring outside, but he doubted very much that they were coming for Junius. He could feel the pistol shot of Junius' words piercing his heart.

"The one true God," he whispered.

"And how do we know that the one true God is our true God when a billion Muslims have their own true God and a billion Christians have their own true God?" Junius said, swaying back and forth, his face ablaze beneath the flickering lights.

"We don't," Needle said.

"That's right," Junius said. "So how do we know we're not a bunch of liars who deserve all the pain and suffering we've gotten?"

"We don't," Needle whispered, remembering his father had sworn on his deathbed that he wasn't sick, that he wouldn't leave his only son for a long, long time.

Needle could feel his faith breaking in that very instant, and he yearned desperately to know the truth, to tear open the heavens and spring headfirst into the lap of God Himself. Needle felt that the answer lay before him and that Junius was the vehicle to take him there. He threw his arms wide and embraced Junius as if he were his own child.

"Let go of me, homo," Junius cried.

He squeezed Junius tighter, felt the bricks of C-4 pressed against his chest, the boy's heart pounding with fury behind the explosive vest. "I believe in God," Needle whispered, as the boy struggled to get away. "There is no other. " And then he saw light tearing through his eyes, like the first blush of morning on the horizon, strung through with a never-ending darkness.

My Darling
Sweetheart Baby

Schultz sat on his front stoop, waiting for the delinquent spring sun to reach his side of the street. It was early April, and despite the Yankee game blaring from a neighbor radio, a winter chill hung heavily in the air. A lot had happened since Schultz had thrown out his back at work and taken disability: his neighbor dog, Buddha, had fallen off the roof and thudded onto the pavement with a final high-pitched yelp; the tinsmith who worked out on the sidewalk sheared off a finger while fitting aluminum for a deli sign; Jimmy Dolan, who Schultz had known since fourth grade, returned from jail and threw a party that lasted till 5:00 a.m. Lately, Jeannie had been stopping by to talk.

"Hey, Schultzie. How's about a beer," she'd say.

"Sure thing," he'd say and amble inside to grab two cold ones. "You seen the new Duane Reade up on Ninth?"

"Naw," she'd say.

"It's got the front of an old bank, with the stone statues underneath the roof pulling faces."

"I guess their mothers didn't tell 'em their faces would stay that way," she'd laugh.

"I'll show you sometime."

Schultz would sip his beer, looking at Jeannie's long neck, listening to her deep breathing, and think: this is the good life, this is what I missed out on all those years I spent slowly breaking my back for a lousy paycheck.

Her eyes could kill you they were so blue. Her buttery brown hair reached halfway down her back. There were times Schultz had wanted to grab a handful, breathe in Jeannie's scent, and stay there all day.

But Jeannie never hung around long; she was always off somewhere in a hurry.

The dark shadows began to ebb and the asphalt at the far edge of the street flamed as an eighteen-wheeler marked LIBERTY OIL rolled past and blasted its horn for the garage down the block to open the gate. The buds were late arriving, and the thin ailanthus trees stood bare along the length of the street. Schultz shivered in his shirt sleeves.

Sometimes Jeannie was off with some guy from another street, or another neighborhood. Sometimes, Schultz thought, they were men from the city. He knew Jeannie could take care of herself, had seen her punch a Puerto Rican in the nose when she was a coltish high schooler at Saint Saviour; made him bleed like a mother. But, every now and then, Schultz felt the urge to cover her tender shoulders with a jacket as she rounded the corner, pulled along by her date.

Schultz caught sight of himself in the smeared glass of his apartment building's front door. Thirty-eight years old. He had been called handsome, but not in a long time. His skin was sickly winter white, and hung loosely around his jaw. He needed a shave, though he'd already shaved that morning. His eyes looked sleepy and everything he saw through those eyes seemed frayed at the edges. His nose was strong and straight – his best feature – but what can you get for a nose? His hair was coming out in the shower, but his scalp was still covered with a mat of spiny, graying hair. His body was a wreck. Before he pulled his back at work he could bench three hundred pounds.

The Yankees scored and the cheering of the crowd brought Schultz back to the street.

Maybe today the check will come.

Schultz had been waiting every day since January for his settlement check to arrive. He knew the postman by name and Schultz sat outside every morning waiting for him to wheel his heavy bag down the street. Schultz felt something close to butterflies in his stomach every time he called out, "Manny, tell me the truth. You gonna make me rich?"

"Not today," Manny'd say, laughing as he stuffed the other five mailboxes. "Why don't you go back to work and get rich?"

"My back's gone. You want I should lift another finger?" he'd say, tilting a can of beer to his mouth.

"You're charmed, Schultzie. You know that?"

"Gimme a break," Schultz would reply.

On those days Jeannie didn't come, his heart felt like the half-choked remnants of last night's dinner. An overwhelming sadness filled him. Lethargy filled him like lead.

He stared at the tattered flags drooping damply from window boxes across the street, their stars and stripes faded to a filmy gauze; the graffiti sprayed haphazardly on the walls of an empty brownstone: COLDASS MARY BITE'S THE BIG ONE. He heard the long, low moan of a tug crawling up the canal.

He had kissed Jeannie once, in a rainstorm. She had taken off her heels and was splashing in puddles, kicking water around, singing some show tune Schultz remembered his mother playing on her stereo when he was a child. It was a quick snap of a kiss, but long enough for Schultz to feel her breath enter him and knock around inside. He felt full of her all day. And when he slept, she was still with him.

Recently, Schultz had asked Jeannie about the kiss.

"We kissed once," Schultz said.

"Did we?" Jeannie said.

"C'mon."

"Really," she said, smiling. "I'm not sure."

"Don't crack my nuts, Jeannie. We kissed."

"Yeah. Where?"

"On the mouth."

"Was it that time in the rain?"

"Yeah. It was that time in the rain."

"Aw, I was drunk, Schultzie."

"But we kissed."

"Yeah, we kissed."

"So, it counts, right?"

"Yeah, it counts."

"Get outta here, ya bum," a voice shouted, and a heavy door slammed shut to Schultz's right.

"You get outta here."

"Clean yerself up, junkie," the voice responded through an open window.

"No, you clean yerself up. You clean yerself up."

Hank Polniaszeki's kid, Hank Jr., bounded down the steps of the neighboring apartment house. He was a couple of years younger than Schultz and like Schultz, he lived in a one-bedroom apartment, two floors above his parents and his childhood home. He wore his hair cropped short so his scalp showed through. He ground his jaw incessantly.

"How ya doin'?" he called across to Schultz, "How ya doin'?"

The sun was finally bleeding onto their side of the street and Schultz could see Hank Jr.'s golden crucifix gleaming against his bare chest. He wore an open jean jacket, jeans and a pair of worn cowboy boots.

"Still waitin'."

"He ain't comin' no faster," Hank Jr. said, holding out his crucifix. "Wit' you sittin' there like a stoop."

"Aw, c'mon."

"You seen Jeannie meenie mincy moe?"

"No, why?" Schultz said.

"I seen her," Hank said, stepping close, his hand tapping on the low wrought-iron fence that fronted their two apartment buildings. "Jeannie's out of her bottle." Schultz noticed for the first time that Hank's teeth were short and sharp, like bits of broken glass.

"I seen her whoring out on Third Avenue."

"Come off it. Take that back, Hank."

"It's the God's honest truth."

"Yer fulla shit. Enough already."

"Ya know she's a whore."

"And I know yer a fuckin' crackhead."

"And yer a loser, Jew, cripple. So basically we's all fucked."

"Say that again," Schultz said, moving to stand. But his back locked up on him and he shot back down onto the cold cement stairs.

"I mean it. I'm tryin' to help you. Forget about her. Ya wanna get crabs, the clap, AIDS, huh?"

"She ain't no whore."

"That's right. She's yer darling sweetheart baby. She whispers sweet nothin's in yer ear, brings you slippers at night, tucks you into bed and kisses yer forehead. She's the most beautiful woman in the freakin' world."

"Shuddup. You just want her."

Hank moved his face as close to Schultz as he could and laughed. "I've had her," he said, spreading his arms wide, "everybody's had her."

"Why don't you go walk yer dog," Schultz said, cracking his knuckles.

"Leave Buddha and the whore alone, God rest his soul. See ya round." Hank stalked down the street, then turned and added, "Ya dumb fuck."

A jaundiced yellow light filled the street. School kids played ball on the road, dodging the cars and cursing as they passed. Schultz was on his fourth beer. The empty cans stood sentry along the low wall to his right, taking sunlight on their dented flanks. Schultz had determined that he loved Jeannie through and through, and that he was going to tell her the truth once and for all. But he needed that check first, as protection, as armor against potential defeat. Schultz didn't win very often, but the thought of the check made him feel like less of a schmuck for once, filled him with hope and promise of a new beginning. He tried to whistle a cheery, spring-like tune, but someone called out for him to "Shuddup."

The mailman started his slow descent down the slope of the street. Schultz slid forward on the step and trained his head towards the distant mailbag. For several minutes, the bag sat unattended on the sidewalk in front of a six-story apartment building.

Schultz felt vaguely deflated when he realized that the figure moving towards him wasn't Manny, who walked with a confident, upright swagger, his broad face open for conversation. The impostor inched down the street, face hidden, shoulders drawn in, never once looking left or right.

Schultz wanted to call out, "You gonna make me rich today?" but he stopped short when he saw that the mailman had thick padded headphones pressed to his ears. He stepped past Schultz as if Schultz were a trash bin, opened the door and filed the mail into its slots.

"Prick," Schultz said, but the mailman didn't hear as he moved on down the street.

Schultz fumbled with the tiny, flat key to his mailbox; it slipped through his fingers to the ground. As he bent to retrieve the key, Schultz felt his insides congeal, a tight band of fire squeeze around his head. He inserted the key and opened the box. A single white, cellophane-windowed envelope dropped out.

The check.

He tore open the envelope. Schultz held the check out in front of him at full arm's length with astonished awe, fingering only its edges, as if it were a bomb about to explode.

Nobody's going to jerk me around now, he thought, inspecting the check.

This is the real thing.

Schultz's mother brought him a jacket to wear and a tuna fish sandwich for dinner. He ate it on the stoop as the streetlights came on, casting a murky glow onto the parked cars and the street below. Church bells rang out a few blocks away, clanging their dissonant tune for a long time. *CLANG-CLANG*, they went. *Christ the King is coming, CLANG-CLANG*. With the check neatly folded in his back pocket, Schultz felt on the verge of bursting with anticipation. He had never seen so many zeroes on a check before. He couldn't wait to tell Jeannie about it. She's probably on the train back from the city now, Schultz thought, though he had had the same thought four times already throughout the day.

Then he saw her turn the corner from the R train, wearing a short leather skirt and high-heeled shoes. He waved to her, but she didn't see him as she bent to tighten a strap on her shoe. When she straightened, Schultz was sure he saw her untwist her underwear beneath her skirt. Schultz felt a sudden sense of wonder, sharing this private moment with Jeannie, like watching her do her business on the toilet. It seemed so natural and comfortable that Schultz wanted to take her in his arms and kiss her, like he had that night in the rain. Another kiss like that would last him the rest of his life.

"How you doin', doll?" Schultz called out.

"Don't doll me. It's been a long day."

Schultz could see Jeannie's face set hard – her fierce war paint newly applied to her lips and cheeks and lashes.

"What happened?"

"Don't ask," she said, lighting a cigarette. She sat on the stoop next to Schultz. She smelled sweet, like some kind of flower.

"C'mon, that'll kill you," Schultz said. "Put it out."

"What the fuck do I care I die?"

"Naw, Jeannie, naw," Schultz said softly. "Things'll be okay."

"Yeah," she said laughing. "Right."

Next door Hank Sr. and his wife, Cele, were shouting. Across the street, a TV was blaring.

"Hey, Jeannie. I got good news."

"Yeah?" she said, through a cloud of smoke.

"Come upstairs."

"Naw, Schultzie. Not tonight."

"Yeah, tonight. I'll make nice. Promise." Schultz paused, "I got beer."

"Yeah, okay," she said after a long moment. She flicked her cigarette into the street in a high, burning arc.

Schultz's apartment smelled of solitude, of empty pizza boxes stacked up by the front door, of unclean laundry and mildewy shower tiles. Jeannie had been up about three or four times since Schultz had stopped work, and she always commented on the posters tacked up in the hall. She especially liked the one with the blue water and sandy beach, Greek ruins in the background. She said it was "romantical." Schultz flicked on an overhead fluorescent light. She followed him to the living room.

"Close your eyes," Schultz said.

"Naw. C'mon."

"Close 'em. It's a surprise."

"Really? It really is?" Jeannie asked, putting her hands over her eyes dramatically.

With the check in his sweating hand, Schultz felt his muscles relax. He felt his heart beating in time for the first time in a long time; it was more than just a throbbing piece of fat after all.

The point of Jeannie's pink tongue jutted out and licked the corner of her mouth. Her nose twitched.

"Can I open my eyes now?"

"Not yet," Schultz said.

His eyes followed the curve of her neck down to the place between her breasts. They were firm and round, though smaller than Schultz was used to. He didn't mind, though. Her pierced belly was flat and beige from the tanning salon. A thin line of downy blond disappeared beneath the waistband of her skirt.

"Now?" she asked. "Can I open 'em now?"

She had never looked so small to Schultz. Her painted toenails looked like shiny candies.

He snapped the check tight in his hand and held it out at eye level for Jeannie to see.

"Okay."

At first, she looked confused. Then saw that he was holding the check.

"Omygawd," she screamed in a high register. "Jesusfuckingchrist." She threw herself into Schultz's arms. The check fell to the floor.

He held her tight, feeling the warmth of her body against his. Her hair smelled like a different kind of flower than her neck did.

"What are you gonna buy me?" she asked, pulling away and doing a pirouette. "Fur? Jewels?"

Schultz could hear pigeons cooing loudly in the air shaft.

"I thought we'd get away from here," Schultz said in a thin voice.

"What do you mean? Like take a trip or somethin'?" Jeannie's smile was starting to sink.

"Jeannie," Schultz said. The name felt holy on his tongue. "Jeannie. I mean you an' me. Let's get outta here. Move to Jersey, go down the shore. Make a new go of it. What do you say?"

"Schultzie, you're kiddin', right?" Jeannie said. "This is a joke, right? I'm not moving nowhere. This is my home. I'm a Brooklyn girl."

The pigeons cooing in the air shaft seemed to be laughing at Schultz. *Coo-coo-roo, coo-coo-roo.* He stepped closer to Jeannie, feeling a twinge in his back, and reached out a hand to touch her. She jumped back, so she was pressed against the wall.

"Don't, Schultzie," she said.

"I don't mean to scare you," Schultz said. "I just wanna say you don't have to do that no more. You don't have to go with those guys an' do that."

"Do what?" Jeannie said. Her eyes were as hard as Lincoln pennies. "Do what? You callin' me a whore, Schultzie? Huh?"

"Come off it, Jeannie. I ain't callin' you nothin'."

"Bullshit. Say it, Schultzie."

"Naw. Nothing, Jeannie."

"That's right, Schultzie, never say nothin' about nothin'. Well, let me tell you, I ain't no Miss Lonelyhearts waiting for no knight in shining armor to save me. You wanna move out to Jersey, it's your funeral. I'm stayin' put right here."

The flickering light suddenly seemed to be too bright, and Schultz realized he had an enormous erection pushing against the zipper of his jeans. Jeannie's face seemed cracked where her foundation was flaking. He craned his neck to kiss her.

She turned her cheek and whispered, in a voice full of tenderness and frailty, "I'm your friend."

But he wasn't listening. He slipped his hand up under her skirt and felt dampness between her legs. She wants it bad, he thought, sliding his finger inside.

"Stop, Schultzie. I don't wanna do this."

"Why not?" he said. "This is what you do, right?"

He cupped her from behind with his free hand and pushed his finger farther inside.

"Stop," she said. "No." Her voice was quiet. "No."

This time, Schultz stopped and slid his finger out, but the smell of her briny sex only inflamed him more.

Her breathing was heavy and her chest heaved.

"Listen, Schultzie. Why don't I go home and come back tomorrow?"

"You won't come back."

"I will," she pleaded. "You know I will."

"Jeannie, take it easy. You gotta be somewhere important?"

She shook her head.

He saw the check lying on the floor, half crumpled from the force of her embrace, and bent to pick it up.

"Tell you what. A check is as good as money. If it's okay by you, I'll give you the whole check, no questions asked. Even-steven."

A flicker of tears came into her eyes. "Naw. I don't wanna do this. I don't want your money."

"I'm as good as the others. I swear I'm good, Jeannie."

"Don't call me Jeannie, okay?"

He lifted her to the bed, and though she wasn't heavy and didn't kick, his back burned like an electrical fire.

"Keep your shoes on," he said, reaching for a pillow. "How do you like it?"

Jeannie shook her head. "You're not going to rape me."

"No," Schultz said, "I wouldn't do that to you," and pressed the check into her hand as he kissed her pulsing wrist.

He undid his belt and slid his pants down. He entered her, and as he thrust himself in and out, his back felt torn and shredded down to his very organs. He felt her tense around him, a live human body, warm, weeping, whispering his name, her eyes open, his face reflected in them, and as she breathed out "Schultzie, Schultzie," he realized that he understood her like no one else; he heard in those words something that the streets had taken from her, a love she could never admit. As he came and dropped heavily onto her keening body, he felt that he'd never be lonely again.

The Miracle Birth

For Shaindy Rudoff, z"l

Shira Bavli wept fervent tears of joy when her daughter, Vered, was born just one week shy of Shira's fortieth birthday. She knew it was a miracle that this tiny tangle of life had sprouted from her wasted womb that had been as parched and Godforsaken as the lunar landscape of the Ramon Crater. Perhaps it was the medications she had taken for her labor pains, but she felt as if a great light had been extracted from her belly.

Eighteen harvests had come and gone since she had married the farmer, Beni Bavli, and their friends and neighbors at Kibbutz Yizhar all had children of their own, most pushing forth an heir and a spare in rapid succession. The Perlman twins would be inducted into the army that fall, snot-nosed Mati Grossman would follow in the spring. It had been a lonely life for Shira and Beni, but that was about to change forever.

The doctor slapped the newborn on its bottom to facilitate the first breath of life, but rather than cry out, the baby laughed, Shira was sure, her tiny round face mocking her with singular intensity.

Kibbutz life can be very cruel, especially if you have secrets to hide. The entire dining hall knew that septuagenarian, Yakov S., was still a hopeless virgin, having survived Buchenwald only to find himself leading a solitary living death in his one-room cottage, and that Izzy Friedlander had pleasured himself into the silken mouths of the spotted dairy calves while his wife slept with the tattooed Russian gardener. They knew that Itamar Blank had ditched reserve duty, claiming a recurrence of the shingles to complete a novel that would never be published, and that Rita Melamed had been caught by the IBA fraudulently text messaging over a thousand votes for her favorite singer on *A Star Is Born*. The members of Yizhar made great sport of these stories, but Shira was loath to entertain such scurrilous gossip. She knew what was being said about her: that she was being punished for sleeping with that boy from Uum Khalil all those years ago, and that she had trapped Beni Bavli into marriage by falsely claiming that she was pregnant with his child. When Beni had discovered the truth about the Arab boy, Shira applied for an abortion and was approved. The irony was not lost on the members of Kibbutz Yizhar, and they were always quick to remind Shira of the upcoming birthday celebrations of their assorted offspring.

But Shira loved Beni and wanted nothing more than to have his child. They tried everything from counting the days of her cycle, to newfangled ovulation tests, to hormone therapy and faddish diets. They tried in vitro fertilization, massage and acupuncture, but nothing worked. Shira even suggested finding a kabbalist, but Beni said she must be losing her mind if she thought one of those maniac magicians could create life. She dreamt of the child most nights, but in her dreams it had a hump like a camel and brayed like a mule.

"Ten fingers, ten toes, one nose," the doctor said, snipping the umbilical cord. "A beautiful, healthy baby."

The child was an angel, the most beautiful thing Shira had ever laid eyes on. And she smiled at the delicious revenge she and Beni would have at the expense of the other kibbutzniks.

"You're laughing," Beni said.

"I'm a mother," she cried. "I'm a mother."

Once, on a visit to Jerusalem, Shira had spotted an Orthodox woman shouting angrily at her five children as they played about before the shining shop windows of Ben Yehuda Street. It's not fair, Shira thought. If only I could have one for my own. She threw herself into Beni's arms and cried; the pain was like that of a humming beehive that had been stirred awake inside her belly.

"I'm old, a useless old sponge," Shira said. "I'm no wife, and you're a fool. Why don't you leave me?"

"You are my wife," Beni said, adding hopefully, "We can adopt."

"What? A Falasha? A gangster Russian? I'd never hear the end of it."

"A baby's a baby," Beni said.

"I want a baby of my own, not somebody's second-hand castoff."

A beggar in a tattered black suit approached, petitioning for *tzedakah*, but Shira chose to ignore him, and return to her own grief. Shira felt a tap on her shoulder. "*Nu?*" the beggar said, smiling, as if he knew the answer to a great secret. "You want to have a child?"

"*Oy va voy!*" she screamed. "I'm going crazy in this lunatic asylum. Is nothing private?" Every time Shira came up to Jerusalem, she realized that the gravitational pull in this impossible city was a hundred times that of the rest of the world, rendering even the simplest encounter as heavy as a stone cut from Solomon's Quarries.

"My wife is upset," Beni said. "Go away."

"A child is a blessing," he persisted. "We must be fruitful and multiply or else Hitler will win."

"Enough with Hitler already," Beni said, lighting a cigarette. "He's burning in hell. We won."

"And yet, you are barren." The beggar pointed a long finger at Shira. "The Tree of Life ends with you."

His words wounded more than they should have, and Shira felt herself buckle, as if punched in the belly.

"Go back to the ghetto and hang yourself from the Tree of Life," Beni shouted. "My wife is none of your business."

"The future of the Jewish people is."

"Ach, you're insane," Beni said, dismissing him with a furious stream of cigarette smoke aimed directly at the beggar's bearded face.

"You are unclean," the beggar said.

"Good," Beni retorted, pulling Shira by the arm.

But the beggar was not pointing at Beni, who had dried cow shit on his work boots and sharp stubble on his face; he was clearly indicating Shira, who, in the refracted afternoon light, could feel his deep black eyes multiplying on her body.

The beggar persisted, following after them, calling Shira spiritually unclean, possessor of a night-black soul. She wrestled herself from Beni's grip. Was there some truth in the beggar's words? During the endless midday hours when the sun was at its highest and she cast no shadow on the earth, she often imagined that her soul had parted from her body and that she had become unmoored from herself, dissociated from time and place. It was then that she returned in memory to the steaming banana fields and Hassan thrusting between her thighs as the cry of muezzins circled from the surrounding hilltops.

"Go to *mikveh* and immerse yourself in its living waters, and you will be blessed," the beggar called.

"Fucking missionaries," Beni said, flicking his cigarette after the beggar who had turned his attention to a pair of tourists drifting out of a shop. "You'd think it would be enough that we live on the land and that we are not out blowing up Jews."

Shira nodded her head sadly and took her husband's hand. She may not have been killing Jews, but she knew that she was responsible for keeping them from coming into this world. In the end, wasn't that just as bad?

For the first time beneath the buzzing fluorescent lights of the delivery room, the baby cried. Beni calmed her and called her Vered, *shhh*, Vered, *shhh*, and the golden pink newborn was quiet. But Shira felt something move inside her, pressing to get out. She knew that creation was a mysterious thing and that to be rewarded with a second child now would not be out of step with the wonders of the unknown.

"Beni, another one is coming," Shira whispered, almost afraid to say the words aloud. She pushed and pushed and felt her insides kneaded, wrung out, but this time it came quickly, sliding from her like dead weight onto the birthing table.

Shira would have called the placenta Agnon if it had been the boy she had been hoping would emerge to complete the familial set.

It had been Shira's turn to work in the chicken house and a hard drenching rain had swept down through the Jezreel Valley, soaking everything, turning the world to mud. She was hefting a bucket of eggs to the idling Tnuva truck when she slipped on a slick wooden stair and tumbled to the ground. Covered in mud and shit and yolk, she heard laughter piercing through the wet air. Rita Melamed and Dahlia Hersch, those henna-rinsed bitches, fell against each other beneath the corrugated metal awning, doubled over in amusement: "Once again, Shiri's eggs are no good," Rita Melamed sang.

She imagined Rita and Dahlia weeping, their sons kidnapped while hitching a ride home from their military bases in the north, or smashed to pieces by a drunk driver at the Megiddo Junction. Did she really wish her neighbors' children dead? She did not know the answer, and that frightened her.

Several days later, she found herself at the Sisters of Israel Ritual Bath in the nearby city of Afula. She did not tell Beni that she was going to the *mikveh*; he scoffed at any religious ritual, even made a point to eat barbecued pork ribs on Yom Kippur. Once, she had lit Shabbat candles on Friday night and he had blown them out.

"When was your last period?" the *mikveh* lady disinterestedly asked in her Russian-inflected Hebrew, as she searched Shira's body for stray hairs and nail polish, remnants of makeup on her face.

"I don't know," Shira said. "A while ago." She was often late and had learned not to get her hopes up.

"You're trying to have child?"

"Yes. No. I don't know," Shira said.

"Your hips are good size for baby."

"I want a baby, but it doesn't want me," Shira said, feeling insecure in her nakedness as she stood before the fully clothed Russian *mikveh* lady, who had short sausage-like arms and a severe mannish face.

She smiled a silver-toothed smile. "You want baby, you will have baby."

"You don't understand. I don't deserve a baby."

"Ha!" the *mikveh* lady laughed. "You think the Arabs who send their children to blow up our buses are better suited? We have woman, eight, maybe nine months

pregnant come to *mikveh* now. You go in water after her.
Soon you have baby."

In order for the immersion to be kosher, Shira had to
sink her entire body under the surface of the water without touching the sides or the bottom of the pool. She
pulled her knees to her chest and sank beneath the warm
water, feeling it wash over her in an amniotic rush. She
felt as if she had returned to the comforting embrace of
the womb, but just as quickly, she popped back into the
world.

"Good. Kosher. Repeat this prayer."

Shira immersed herself two more times and during
each dunk she reached out for the child that she hoped
was expecting her on the other side of the waters, as if
there were a waiting room lined with babies anxious to be
born. But in the darkness behind her eyelids, she found
only guilt and recrimination. And then, *pop*, like a cork to
the surface.

"Good. Kosher," the *mikveh* lady said, as Shira recited
the prayer. "Remember, if you do not come back soon,
your baby will have face like monkey."

She did not return to the *mikveh* and Vered was born
with Shira's face, a lovely face, smooth, fresh and unlined
from worry, her body the perfect size for cradling, pink as
a Rose of Sharon.

Shira and Beni found themselves welcomed into the
community of parenthood, receiving smiles, gifts, and
advice solicited or not. Their fellow kibbutzniks cried
"*L'Chaim!*" and threw a party that lasted until the stars

faded from the sky. Shira wondered whether Hassan, with his eight children up in the hills, could hear the revelers.

Rita Melamed sheepishly gave Shira her wooden rocking chair, saying that it would help ease the infant into sleep, and Yakov S. offered to teach Vered to speak Yiddish so that it would not disappear entirely from the world. Shira was thankful that she'd had her baby now, at a time when she could appreciate the enormity of her accomplishment and spend time bonding with the baby, rather than packing the infant off to the children's house the way she and Beni and the other adults had been when they were children. She was thankful she could nurse Vered whenever she desired, and watch her breathe quietly as she slept.

But Vered slept restlessly and cried day and night, and by the end of her second year she threw up nearly everything she was fed. The kibbutz nurse said it was nothing more than a protracted case of colic, but Shira knew that it should have passed after a few months.

"Who knew you'd turn into a Polish mother so quickly," Beni laughed.

Sometimes, when Beni was working at the new perfume factory that had supplanted the chicken house at the north end of the kibbutz, Shira would cradle Vered in her arms, rock her back and forth and pray that she would live a long healthy life. With her fingers she traced the lines on her daughter's palms and felt comforted. "My soul," she whispered in the child's ear, "I love you."

Despite her difficulties keeping down food, Vered did not lose weight. In fact, her soft body had the texture of slowly rising dough. She did not look ill to the kibbutzniks, who marveled at the rosy glow of her skin. One evening after supper, Yakov S. asked if he could hold the child, a film of tears filling his eyes as he breathed, almost inaudibly, *"Gei scluffen bubeleh."*

After she learned to walk, Vered was quick to complain, *"Ima,* I'm tired."

The kibbutz boys, awkward and insecure among girls their own age, fell over each other offering to carry Vered on their backs, a personal shuttle service for the most beautiful black-eyed child they had ever seen. Tal Hersch fashioned Vered a tinfoil crown to wear exclusively when he was at her service, and Reuven Friedlander promised he would marry her one day.

Shira and Beni argued.

"Maybe she's allergic," Shira screamed one evening. "You come back from that perfume factory smelling like a whorehouse. Maybe it's those chemicals you mix all day. Who knows what you put into those potions."

"It's all in your head. Vered is fine. She's been tested for every disease, every allergy, everything. The doctor says there's nothing wrong with her."

"A country doctor."

"Do you want there to be something wrong with her? Is that it? Because if you keep looking hard enough, you will find something. She is happy. The boys like her. One has already proposed marriage to her."

"She is three-and-a-half years old, and the Friedlander boy has Asperger's syndrome."

"Well, what do you want me to do?"

"I want her to see a specialist."

Beni lit a cigarette. "That would make you happy?"

"It depends."

· They took Vered to Rambam Hospital in Haifa and ran her through a series of MRIs, CAT scans, ultrasounds, X-rays and blood tests. Dr. Goldgraber marveled at her startling beauty, commenting that Vered was a vision from heaven. But her blood work was abnormal and the MRI revealed something that the doctor was hard-pressed to explain. "There is a mass," he said, carefully selecting his words.

Shira clapped her hands to her face.

"Not a tumor. The blood work is not consistent with that, but there is a foreign body about the size of a grape in her belly."

"Does she have cancer?" Shira grasped Beni's hand, and then nudged him. "Say something."

"My wife wants to know if it is cancer."

"No, no," the doctor chuckled. "It looks to me like nothing more than an extra mass of tissue, completely benign. Many people live with tumors much larger than this for years and live completely healthy lives."

"But you said it's not a tumor. What should we do? My baby."

"I'll be honest with you. I don't know what it is, but it doesn't look serious right now."

"What about the blood tests?" Shira asked.

"Shira, the doctor says she is fine," Beni said.

"What is wrong with her blood?" she demanded. "Is it Tay-Sachs? Canavan?" She was certain that the fetus she had aborted had been safe from that cursed cocktail of genes. But her and Beni? She had no idea.

"Please don't worry about that. We have tested for all the appropriate diseases," the doctor said. "Some of her hormone levels are a little high. But they can vary from person to person. Just keep an eye on her, and if anything changes, we can always have the tissue surgically removed."

As absurd and irrational as it sounded to Shira, she determined that the *mikveh* lady had put the evil eye on beautiful Vered as punishment, given that Shira had disregarded the lady's ominous insistence that Shira return to the baths. Vered continued to grow by the day, but she did so with such languid torpor that Shira became mad with worry; the other children her age ran and played while Vered sat in stately conference with Yakov S., speaking a dead language as the older girls fell over each other for the privilege to braid Vered's long black hair.

The Sisters of Israel Ritual Bath stank of chlorine, and Shira held tight to Vered's hand as she searched for the *mikveh* lady. A dark, gaunt woman, who carried herself with a stern military bearing, appeared before them.

"I'm looking for a woman, Russian, I think," Shira said.

"There is no Russian here."

"She is the *mikveh* lady."

"She is gone," the woman said with finality.

Shira told the woman that she had been barren and had come to the *mikveh* and immersed herself after a pregnant woman, that she'd then become pregnant herself.

"*Bubbe meysehs*," the woman laughed. "You think the Russian turned you into a living *matryoshka* doll? You were probably pregnant when you came here. Or maybe the waters simply unclogged your tubes." She laughed again.

"She said that if I did not return, something terrible would happen to my daughter."

"And has it?"

"I don't know."

"Hi, sweetie," the woman said, turning her attention to Vered. "She is more beautiful than Queen Esther. I would not worry about her."

"Please," Shira pleaded. "Please. There's something wrong with her."

"This is your first child?"

"Yes."

"Let me tell you, as a Jewish mother, that there's something wrong with every child who doesn't completely match our impossible expectations."

"You don't understand. Please, let the waters of the *mikveh* purify her."

"No." The woman looked as if she had been slapped in the face. "You cannot put a child into the *mikveh*, not until she is to be married, otherwise she is exposed to the sexual advances of any man."

As she continued to grow older, Vered spent more and more time conversing in Yiddish with Yakov S. while the boys, burning with jealousy, stood outside his garden. Vered's black hair now reached below her waist.

Shira scolded Yakov S. to stop feeding Vered. "She's getting fat. I know you have known deprivation, but that does not mean you should spoil my child."

The phone rang first thing Sunday morning; an American was on the line speaking a stilted Hebrew.

"English is okay," Shira said.

He told her that his name was Jay Rubenstein and that he was a medical student at the Technion in Haifa. "I've been working with Dr. Goldgraber," he said. "And I've been looking over some of the recent test results."

Shira felt all the breath exit her body at once. To her, an American meant can-do know-how and authority, even if he was only a student. "What is it?" she said.

"This is rather strange, but all the evidence I see here – the highly elevated HCG and progesterone levels, and the latest ultrasound results are consistent with the end of the first trimester of pregnancy. I don't know why Dr. Goldgraber didn't pick this up."

"What?" Shira laughed. "What sort of joke is this?"

"Your daughter is sixteen years old?"

"She is six years old."

"Six?" There was silence on the other end of the line. "Pregnancy at this age is a medical impossibility.

Perhaps you were meant to have twins and the second fetus found its way into the first. It's not unheard of. Of course, with so many hormones and steroids in the food supply these days, puberty is sometimes accelerated by several years. Anything is possible. Now, this may be a sensitive question, but has anyone touched your daughter in an inappropriate manner?"

Shira stormed over to Yakov S.'s secluded cottage out by the perimeter fence; who knew what kind of debauchery went on in there? She should have never trusted him, virgin or not. She hammered on the door with her fists. "Open up, you pervert. Open up now."

A moment later, a frail and haggard Yakov S. appeared at the door. His eyes were milky and his lips were cracked. His room was gloomy and smelled of musty books and stale air.

"Where is my daughter?"

"She is sitting over there drinking tea."

Vered sat by a small window sipping from a cup.

"Come with me right now."

"But, *Ima*, I'm learning about the Fools of Chelm."

"Ach. These stories reek of the *shtetl*. Why would you teach her about an ugly, horrible, dead world?"

"You don't understand. She is special."

"She is my daughter. I know she is special." Shira demanded that Vered leave Yakov S.'s house at once.

"But *Ima*—"

"Enough. You should not be drinking tea alone with a dirty old man." Then she turned to Yakov S. and shrieked, "What did you put in my daughter's tea? Come with me, Vered. Now."

But her daughter looked to Yakov S. and muttered something in Yiddish that Shira could not understand.

"Vered, you should go," Yakov S. said. "If your mother wishes."

Shira grabbed Vered by the arm and pulled her towards the door. "You will never come back here again," she scolded.

"Shiri, let me explain," Yakov S. said. He looked thin and weak and the few hairs left on the top of his head stood up as if electrified by static.

"Another time."

"I will be gone soon," he said sadly.

"You are leaving the kibbutz?"

"This world," he said.

"Okay," she said. "Speak."

Yakov S. smiled a vague, sickly smile; the contours of his skull were clearly visible beneath his thin, papery skin. "I know that Vered is pregnant, that she was born pregnant; this may be difficult for your rational mind to understand, but every generation has a potential messiah, someone from the House of David who promises to rise up and lead the Jewish people. Yes, there have been false messiahs. But there have also been true messiahs who have sadly gone to their deaths anonymously."

"Nonsense," Shira laughed.

"How do you think a child became pregnant? Surely you don't think—"

"I don't ever want her coming back here."

"You fear your own redemption," Yakov S. said, in a voice tinged with sadness.

"*Ima*, I am the Sabbath Bride," Vered said brightly.

"Is that what this pervert told you? Where did he touch you?"

"Once in a generation," he continued.

"Folk tales, old world *dybbuks*."

"I have seen the Sabbath Bride before; she lived in my village. She was too beautiful for any man, yet she became pregnant. She glowed with celestial light. I was young and I loved her, everyone loved her, she was so beautiful. She promised herself to my friend Itzik, but birth pangs of the Messiah last for many years, and before she was eighteen, ripe and ready to burst with life, a German shot her in the head and the belly. My family, friends, my entire village was exterminated that day."

"You told this to my daughter?"

"Yes. So we will never forget."

"You told my six-year-old daughter of murder, bloodshed and massacres? It is no wonder she cannot sleep at night. You have been filling her head with nightmares."

"You do not understand," Yakov S. said.

"You don't understand," Shira said. "She is a little girl."

"With the fate of the world in her belly."

"Nonsense," Shira said, and pushed open the door leading to Yakov S.'s fragrant garden. "You will never speak to my daughter again."

As she tugged Vered down the stone pathway from his house, Shira could see through the early dusk Yakov S. standing in his doorway. He looked lost, as if he didn't know whether he was in this world or the next.

Shira forbade Vered to go to Yakov S.'s funeral, telling her that an eight-year-old girl should be focusing on her studies, not on ghosts of another age.

Beni agreed to stay home and watch Vered while Shira paid her respects at the founder's cemetery in the whispering cypress grove outside the kibbutz fence. Only six people stood out in the wind to bury Yakov S.; after his confrontation with Shira, he had been effectively out-cast from the community. Now, looking down into the small hole in the earth, Shira felt a great sadness that she had done nothing to alleviate the enormous suffering in his life.

Vered had grown strange as her belly expanded, responding to her parents' requests solely in the *mama loshn*. She was effectively a prisoner in her own home. Just the week before, Beni had caught her trying to climb through her bedroom window.

"Why?" Beni pleaded with his daughter. "Do you have to speak that foul language?"

Now, she appeased her father by speaking in Heb-rew. "I have to practice so I can speak to Yakov and his family when they are restored to life."

Shira and Beni took Vered to a psychiatrist for eval-uation. They had just come from the physician, where they had listened to the Doppler test that picked up a heartbeat in Vered's belly. It sounded like a faint running of horses on a windy plain.

The psychiatrist was enchanted by Vered. His ice-blue eyes watched her every gesture as her parents laid out their case that something was seriously wrong with their daughter.

"She thinks the Messiah is going to return and bring the dead to life," Shira said.

"Yes," the psychiatrist said matter-of-factly as he scratched his chin. "The dead will return to life when the Messiah arrives."

"When, you say?" Beni said. "This is make-believe, a child's fantasy."

"That Jews have believed in for thousands of years. Are you questioning the wisdom of our fathers?"

"I question everything," Beni said, flicking his Zippo lighter.

"And isn't it a burden to question the laws of gravity, the cycle of the seasons, when they are unalterable fact?"

"I think you are mad," Beni said.

"This entire country is mad," the psychiatrist said. "Who could have ever imagined that this barren desert land would be repopulated by Jews? Who could have ever imagined that we would survive and thrive even while surrounded by enemies on all sides? Who could have ever imagined that an Israeli, rest his soul, would go into outer space? Sometimes we must simply unbind ourselves from rationality and submit to the manifold mysteries of life."

"You don't understand," Shira said. "My daughter is pregnant and she's losing her mind. She babbles all day in Yiddish and stares out the window like she's waiting for a guest to arrive."

"If you think the pregnancy is making her mad, then you can simply take her for an abortion and be done with it."

"No," Shira said. "No abortion."

"Our daughter will not have an abortion." Beni said.

"When will she have the child? When will we have our daughter back?" Shira pleaded.

"As you know, normal gestation time for humans is nine months," the psychiatrist said, reaching for a book on a shelf behind him. "But metaphysical time operates on an entirely different schedule. In Genesis, it is written that the world was created in seven days. How long did each day last? Twenty-four hours? Surely not. Perhaps each day lasted thousands or millions of years. Vered looks to be about four or five months pregnant. She is nine years old. You do the math."

"Is there anything you can do to help?"

"I can write up a prescription to help you deal with your anxiety."

As a she grew older, Vered was bright and beautiful and charming, and Shira chastised herself for not giving her daughter more credit as a human being. Vered would turn out all right in the end, just as Shira had. When her mother asked if the baby was moving, Vered lifted her shirt and placed Shira's hand on her thrilling belly.

After school Vered worked at the new travelers' restaurant that had replaced the communal dining hall in the center of the kibbutz. Her belly was large now, and she shone like something on fire. Her straight black hair swept across diners' tables as she twirled past. A group of Protestant pilgrims visiting the biblical site of Megiddo gave her gifts they had brought from the American heartland. She thanked them and laughed her gypsy laugh, wild and full of flashing teeth. Her English had become almost native and she often entertained travelers, spinning tales about golems and the Fools of Chelm.

"One more, Scheherazade, one more!" they'd cry.

One night, a lone sojourner from Tzfat on his way to visit Joseph's Tomb in Shechem called her to his table. "Where is your husband?"

"I'm only fifteen years old," she blushed.

"So you are not married?"

"No," she said.

Shira saw the man lean in and whisper something into Vered's ear. She wordlessly nodded her head and went about cleaning tables.

Not long after that night, Shira began to notice that the cloying scent of the factory's perfume clung to Vered's skin like a patina, bouquets of it following her every move.

She asked Beni if Vered had been coming to visit him at the factory but he said no. Months passed and Shira could not figure out why her daughter stank of the pre-fabricated fragrances created in the kibbutz laboratories;

Vered kept no perfume at home and the girls her age had grown distant and whispered about her when she passed.

One night, as Shira lay awake in bed worrying about her daughter – who seemed on the verge of bursting, and often disappeared for hours at a time, God knows where – she heard a soft tapping at her window. There, through the glass, Shira saw the anguished face of the handsome young South African investor who had been staying at the guesthouse that past week as he negotiated with the kibbutz elders about acquiring their fragrances for his company.

"Vered," he pleaded. "I must see you again."

In his voice, Shira heard Hassan's, and in an instant, she felt the years fall away. "Where?" she said, her stomach stirring with old feelings.

"Behind the factory, as usual."

This is insane, Shira thought as she dressed, Beni snoring lightly at her side. I am an old woman, I will soon be a grandmother. She looked in the mirror and her face was deeply lined with worry, her hair gray and brittle like straw. In her drawer, she found a silken scarf that she had not worn since she was a teenager. She covered her hair with it, so as not to give herself away. She had put on weight over the years, a kilogram one year, two the next, and her soft belly protruded like a woman in her second trimester.

The sky was cloudy and dark, not a star flickered above, and she followed the sweet scent of youth towards the perfume factory. Shira discovered that this was the only place on the kibbutz that did not smell even a little bit like cow shit; it smelled like the Garden of Eden, full of flowers and fruit trees. Though her eyes were not yet accustomed to the dark, she knew that the handsome South African was waiting for her, his breath rising and falling rapidly. Shira's heart pounded loudly in her chest. She was sure he could hear it thumping away.

"My love, I'm so glad you decided to come. I've been sick all day thinking of you."

"Good," Shira said, in a voice that was no longer her own.

"Come to me," he said from the darkness.

"No. You."

It had been a long time since Shira had played this game; her lovemaking with Beni had become so mechanical and automatic that once, she had suggested that he arrange an evening with the milking machine at the dairy to take care of his needs.

"Vered. I need you," he said, his voice boyish and almost apologetic.

"I'm here," Shira said.

He rushed to her in the darkness, threw his arms around her, and kissed her hard on the lips. As they kissed, Shira felt she was being reborn, given a second chance on the life she had fouled up. They dropped to the ground and Shira pulled him closer by his broad muscular back.

"You're so beautiful," he said, biting her earlobe.

His stomach was flat and tight and strong, and she wanted to give herself to him. He pressed his cheek to hers, and she pulled away, afraid her skin would betray her.

"I want you," he said, and lifted her skirt.

He was unzipping his pants when Shira heard the unmistakable sound of an IDF helicopter patrolling the skies above the Jezreel Valley. Before she knew it the helicopter, on its way to Jenin perhaps, was passing over them, its bright lights settling for a moment on the South African's chiseled features and on Shira's sunken face.

"What the hell?" the South African said. "Is this some sort of joke?"

"Whore," Shira shouted at Vered the next morning. "You've been sneaking off with strange men behind the perfume factory."

"*Ima*," she said blithely. "They're not strange."

"Like a wild beast, you're doing it with every man who will have you."

"Like mother like daughter. At least I don't have to worry about getting pregnant."

Shira slapped her across the cheek.

Vered laughed in Shira's face and spat out a colorful string of obscenities. "Yes. Hit the mother of the Messiah. It's a wonderful idea."

"You really believe that nonsense, don't you?"

"What else can explain a sixteen-year pregnancy? I feel him inside me like an iridescent fish. All the wisdom of all the ages grows in my belly, and you worry about some harmless sex, because you are so unhappy in your life."

"I am not unhappy."

"Tell me," Vered said. "Tell me you wouldn't switch places with me if you had the chance."

"Vered, you're a sick girl. Your beauty has blinded you to the facts. There is no Messiah."

"You have no faith that tomorrow can be better," Vered said. "So life is a misery."

Shira and Beni divorced shortly afterwards; she confessed the details of her humiliation with the South African, and admitted to her endless fantasies of Hassan, her unhappiness in the bedroom. She could not go on any longer. Beni quietly packed his belongings into a truck and moved to Tel Aviv as if he had been waiting all along for the excuse to leave.

Now, Shira had no one but her daughter. Vered's rising blood pressure and swollen ankles sentenced her to constant bed rest in anticipation of the baby's birth. Shira brought her food, bathed her and brushed her long hair. For the first time in a long time, Shira felt like a mother instead of a prison warden.

It was the spring of Vered's eighteenth year. Her belly was high and rounded like a golden sand dune, and every once in a while a foot or hand was visible through the thin curtain of skin. Knees and elbows bulged. At one point, Shira was sure she could see the contours of a tiny face.

Shira felt that with the birth of this child her suffering would finally be over, a vindication of her daughter's endless pregnancy. "Vered," she said, as she stroked her daughter's hair. "I have always been sorry that I forbade you to see Yakov S. He was a harmless old man, and I treated him like a criminal. It is the great regret of my life."

"You didn't know better," Vered said softly. Her skin glowed with a sheen of perspiration. "You didn't know how much I loved him."

"I just wish it had turned out differently."

The contractions were strong and came quickly, and Shira barely had time to get her daughter to the hospital before gushes of amniotic fluid poured from Vered like a flash flood in a *wadi*. Flushed a deep red, body atremble, Vered tore off her hospital gown; she cried and laughed and cried again, cursing the doctor who told her to breathe. And as Vered pushed and her facial expression twisted into a grimace under the exertion, Shira felt that she was looking into her own face; for the first time Shira saw herself in her beautiful daughter. She took Vered's hand in her own and reassured her that everything would be all right.

It wasn't until the baby's head began to emerge from the birth canal that Shira realized she had not called Beni to be present at their grandchild's birth; she hoped someone from the kibbutz had called him and that he was on his way.

The baby appeared, blushing pink and full of light, his face calm and serene beneath a head of curls, his body soft and strong: ten fingers, ten toes, one nose.

When the nurse cleaned up the infant and handed him to Vered, she wept the inconsolable tears of someone who had never known what it felt like to be alone with her own body. Tears poured from her and mixed with those of her child.

When she finally stopped crying, Vered held the baby out for Shira to hold.

"I want to call him Agnon," Vered said.

"What?" Shira said, feeling the baby's warm breath against her cheek.

"You always loved that name, and you never had a boy."

There was a knock at the hospital room door. Shira handed Agnon back to Vered and answered the door, expecting to see Beni's smiling face. Instead, she saw someone she did not recognize. A handsome young man, his thick black hair slicked against his head, wearing a finely tailored suit – out of date, but stylish nonetheless – smiled and entered the room. He held a bouquet of flowers in his hand, and uttered some words that Shira did not understand. And then she heard Vered's response in her practiced Yiddish, and Shira knew that Yakov S. had returned from his wandering.

The Engines of Sodom

Hershlag's mother hit him over the head with a loaf of rye bread when he told her he was going to catch a show at Ildiko's instead of joining her at synagogue to mark his grandfather's *yahrzeit*. "What's the matter with you? Poppa's been gone a year today and you're running downtown to fill your ears with that trash."

Hershlag raised a delicate middle finger, jumped on his skateboard and wobbled down the driveway.

Connor and McManus were crouched on their boards in front of the club sharing a sodden pizza sub when Hershlag rolled up. They had large black X's drawn in marker on the backs of their hands and Hershlag was glad that he had had the foresight to mark himself before his mother went crazy.

In Hebrew school, he had been called Hershlag the Fag by the spoiled Forest Hill JAPs because he had acne and wore Lee, instead of Levi's; the next year, he was a skinhead boozing with Eamon Sturtze and Little John at the Bulldog. Now he didn't drink or smoke and hadn't been to the Bulldog since it had been shuttered following a bloody after-hours brawl.

He wore his high-top sneakers, an oversized *Walk Together, Rock Together* T-shirt and sanctimonious black

X's scrawled onto his skin. "Gonna be a great show tonight, guys. I read in *Maximumrocknroll* that this band shreds."

"You haven't heard them?" McManus sneered.

"Sure I have. Their old stuff."

McManus rolled his eyes at Connor. "What's up with your arms, Hershlag?"

He hadn't had time to throw on long sleeves before his mother chased him out, and now his slim, scarred arms were visible for his new friends to see. It looked like a melon baller had scooped out the tender flesh of his forearms, leaving the wounds to heal into cruel putty-like scars.

"Got rid of some old tattoos," Hershlag said. "Dragons and skulls. Kids' stuff. I'm thinking of getting some new ones, though. You know, a little bit straight and a little bit edgy." He laughed, but his companions did not.

"Hey kids, don't forget your fake IDs," he quipped, trailing after them.

When old man Ildiko introduced the opening band the club was already smoke-filled and packed. Hershlag popped in his earplugs and yelled something to McManus, who was talking up a dreadlocked Asian girl who lived in Kensington Market.

McManus spun around and poked Hershlag in the chest with a stiff finger. "Go away, Hershlag."

Connor scolded McManus and told him not to be so hard on the kid, then disappeared into the rolling wave of bodies.

Amid the clash of distorted buzzsaw guitars, Hershlag thought of his grandfather. Not long before he died, Poppa had approached Hershlag's bedroom. The music was blasting.

"*Oy!*" Poppa Hershlag had shouted. "Like the very engines of Sodom. Turn that racket off, Adam. It will put me in the ground."

Hershlag had laughed at how weak his grandfather's plaintive "*Oy*" sounded compared to the militant, testosterone-fuelled *Oi, oi, oi's* chanted on his record.

Then Poppa Hershlag had seen the tattoos and shaken his numbered arm at his only grandson. "Do you think this is a joke? Does this mean nothing to you? You are a lucky boy, Adam, to be born in the time you were born. Don't ever forget that."

Hershlag's scars itched and he scratched absently at them as the band cleared the stage.

Despite the swelling crowd pressing around him, Hershlag felt a deep loneliness and shame. He missed his grandfather and had done nothing to honor his memory. Poppa Hershlag deserved more than a candle and a muttered prayer.

Connor stumbled up from the mosh pit, sweating through his T-shirt. "I'm going backstage to hang with the band. Wanna come?"

Hershlag nodded and followed Connor through the crowd, but he was stopped by a voice calling, "Look who's back from the dead."

"And with the straight edge crew," a second voice added.

Eamon and Little John stood before Hershlag and Connor in identical oxblood Doc Marten boots, blue jeans and red suspenders snapped tight over their Fred Perry polo shirts. They were a couple years older than Hershlag and towered over him like fully grown men.

Eamon flicked Hershlag in the nose with a battered finger. Eamon's head was newly shaved and a droplet of red blood had dried on the side of his scalp. "I didn't think I'd see your sorry ass again. What happened to your tats? I thought we were brothers." Then he gestured to the swastika tattoo on his forearm, the Death's Head, the SS lightning bolts.

The next band was doing its sound check and Connor had to shout. "You're a Nazi?"

"No, I'm not."

"He's a Jew. How can you miss a nose like that?" Eamon taunted.

Connor shook his blond head and burst through the crowd, shouting in disgust, "A Nazi."

"Oops," Eamon laughed and grabbed Hershlag's skateboard. "I guess you're out of friends, mate."

Hershlag stood a moment, trying to find the right words, but he was afraid that he would cry in front of Eamon and Little John, and nothing – nothing in the world, he was sure – could be worse than that. In an instant, he was running down Bloor Street, in search of the tattoo parlor, giant snot bubbles bursting from his nose. He had his grandfather's blurred blue numbers committed to memory and he was determined to become a living monument to Poppa Hershlag so that Hershlag himself would never forget.

The Madonna of Temple Beth Elohim

Private First Class Jimmy Mahoney was ambushed while on patrol in the restive city of Fallujah and died for nearly two minutes. He never saw the fireball that forever scorched three of his friends' names onto memorial walls in Wood River, Nebraska; North Judson, Indiana; and Newburgh, New York. He never saw the panicked lieutenant pound his chest and breathe life back into him, or the Medevac helicopter that lifted him to the safety of an army hospital in Kuwait. What he saw, he could not say, but he knew that he was saved by the grace of God.

That was what Father Michael Kerslake told his colleague and co-host of the weekly interfaith radio show, *God Matters*, when he called him on the telephone at the beginning of September. Rabbi Josh Kaminski had mentioned weeks earlier that his maintenance man was taking a vacation and that as such, the rabbi needed help setting up the sanctuary for the High Holidays. Jimmy had refused the MDC crossing guard job that Father Kerslake had gotten him near Jimmy's home in Southie, saying the screaming orange vest and Day-Glo band across the hat degraded the memory of his friends who had died in uniform.

"I want him to join the land of living," Father Kerslake had said. "You know, idle hands—"

Temple Beth Elohim was a modern glass and steel structure tucked away in a wooded area no more than a mile from the Charles River. Father Kerslake parked the car and led the way with a determined stiff-legged limp, Jimmy lagging behind. Father Kerslake's hair was white and thin; his pink scalp showed through here and there. "Come on, Jim," he called. His voice was still the rich and sonorous baritone that Jimmy, as a child, had equated with that of God. It was this voice, in fact, that had broken Jimmy's reclusion. For weeks, he had sat slumped on the couch in his pajamas, playing solitaire while the chattering skulls on television squawked about the war. Most days, he felt like he had a cemetery buried in his heart.

Now, the fresh air whispered through the dark places inside of him that hurt to touch, and Jimmy quickened his pace to catch up with Father Kerslake. He had never seen a building that looked like this one; it reminded him of an exercise from a school math book. Scalene triangles, equilateral triangles and isosceles triangles, all represented in a glass structure set on defying the laws of physics. There seemed to be no roof, just sharp, forbidding points where the straight lines met. Jimmy was suddenly afraid to enter this arcane building.

"What does it mean?" Jimmy asked.

"Temple Beth Elohim? It means House of God."

"House of God?" Jimmy mused. "I thought the church was the House of God."

"God's houses are many and blessed are those who enter them with an open heart," Father Kerslake said. "I'll find Rabbi Kaminski."

It was a bright day and light flooded in through the tall, broad windows that narrowed to a fine point at their apex. Jimmy's feet echoed off the tile floor. Not far from the entrance, he found a water fountain next to a glass showcase. Jimmy stood before the glass. A face looked back at him: gaunt and asymmetrical, with large, haunted eyes. It took a moment for him to realize that this image was his own reflection. He leaned in to inspect his transformed face, but the image disappeared before his eyes. The contents of the display case were clear now, and he saw strange occult candelabras, some brass, some silver, one adorned with two-dimensional lions, another shaped like a tree with wild, wandering roots at its base. He saw tiny scrolls peppered with lettering as mysterious and singular as flecks of dust. He saw the twisted horn of a large animal, but could not determine what kind of beast had been sacrificed for this ornament. With his left hand he absently fingered the ribbon of his Purple Heart.

Father Kerslake appeared with the rabbi. "Jimmy, this is Rabbi Kaminski."

"Always a pleasure to meet a war hero." The rabbi extended his hand. "My grandfather fought in the Pacific."

He was younger than Jimmy thought a holy man could be, no older than thirty. His face was clean-shaven and his enormous white teeth forced his lips into an insistent smile. He wore an immaculate blue suit that made Jimmy, in his work shirt and jeans, feel underdressed. "I'm glad you're able to help us out, Jimmy," the rabbi said. "The New Year is the busiest time of year around here. It doesn't look it now, but this place will be packed to the rafters by the end of the week."

"How come there's no roof?" Jimmy asked.

The rabbi smiled and said nothing.

"Jimmy was an apprentice roofer in his family's construction business before he enlisted," Father Kerslake said.

"Oh, so you know roofs – or is it rooves?" the rabbi laughed.

Jimmy had climbed the tall landmark mansions of Beacon Hill and brought light to the pale blue bloods, installing skylights above their darkened attics; he had rubberized the roofs of leaky starter homes and hot-tarred the tops of cookie-cutter townhomes in the suburbs west of Boston. But he had never seen anything like Temple Beth Elohim, slanting upward to the sky like a shining iceberg.

"My brothers won't have me in the business," Jimmy said. "They think I'm no good anymore."

"Jim, you know it's the insurance, the union—" Father Kerslake said.

"Okay," Rabbi Kaminski said. "Why is there no roof? I'll give you two answers. One is practical, the other is, let's say, spiritual. First, New England winters, with all this snow, are killers for roofs, all that dead weight. So the architect figured sharp angles and glass; snow slides right off. But this is what I tell my congregants. With glass walls and windows, nothing is hidden from God. There is nowhere to hide."

"But," Jimmy interjected, "isn't it true that nothing is hidden from God wherever you are? Isn't He supposed to be everywhere?"

The rabbi laughed and Father Kerslake patted Jimmy on the shoulder. "I think you got him, Jim."

"Let's put him to work before he takes my job on the pulpit," the rabbi laughed.

In the synagogue's basement supply closet, Jimmy found a mop and a bucket full of rags and cleaners: a can of Brasso, a plastic jug of industrial disinfectant and a bottle of Murphy Oil Soap. Hirsch, the elderly part-time maintenance man who was on his way to New York to spend the High Holidays with his grandchildren, had left Jimmy a hand-written list of tasks to complete.

The list said:

move wall
put chairs
mop floor
polish brass and wood
bathroom clean to eat off

The light was at its brightest in the sanctuary. Jimmy wondered whether this was due to the blinding effect of emerging from the depths of the basement or if it was because of the triangular prisms above, which seemed to be aiming the force of their light directly at the pulpit like a spotlight. He looked up to the sky and felt blinded by the sharp rays of the September sun. The apex of the synagogue must have been sixty or seventy feet high.

When he had worked as an apprentice up on the steep slanted roofs, Jimmy felt a freedom he had never felt down in the crowded streets of his neighborhood. Up there in the sky, with the sun on his face and the wind riding high around him, he felt alive, in a world of his own, endless with possibility. Sometimes, he could see the tops of birds' wings as they flew past. His friend and mentor, John Fishercat, the master roofer, had taught Jimmy to strip a pitched roof in half the time of the union layabouts, how to spread hot bitumen over the insulation to seal the seams, and how to resize and cut slate without wasting so much as a millimeter. John Fishercat had the scourged face of an old walnut, a silver flat-topped haircut, and rust-colored hands as broad as garden rakes. He claimed he was a pure Pequot Indian whose ancestors had fought in King Philip's War, but, after reaching the bottom of a bottle of Jack Daniels one night, he admitted to Jimmy that his name was really Jean Beaulieu. He was a lapsed Catholic from Lowell who, to avoid paying federal, state and municipal taxes, had taken the social security number and identity of his mentor – a real three-quarters Pequot – after he was hit by lightning.

John Fishercat had taught Jimmy about the Four Cardinal Directions.

It was late autumn; the two men were working a roof. The sun was slowly draining from the sky, and John Fishercat pointed over his shoulder to the fading ball of light.

"When you work, always try to face east."

"What do you mean?" Jimmy had said. He couldn't tell east from west or north from south.

"To the west is death."

"I don't understand."

"East is success, happiness. The sun rises in the east, dies in the west," John Fishercat said, pointing to the darkened sky out above the swaying treetops. "It's rebirth, Jimmy, renewal. The golden eagle flies east. The Jews pray to the east and Jerusalem, the Muslims face east to Mecca, the three wise men came from the east."

"But," Jimmy said, "wouldn't that mean they were walking towards the west?"

John Fishercat had been walking in his namesake's shoes for nearly thirty years and had come to identify with Native American spirituality as if his ancestors' bones were truly scattered across the conquered soil of New England. "Listen to me. Forget the fact that I'm supposed to be a hundred years old. I've seen enough men break their necks in thirty years. North is defeat; south is peace. When you work, face east, or south. Otherwise—" And he snapped a piece of slate in half with his giant fingers.

Jimmy heeded John Fishercat's advice and worked with the morning sun on his face, shifting his body with new-found freedom as the day progressed. The rules were clear: if he did what he was told, nothing could touch him.

Jimmy did not know what direction he was facing when the insurgent's RPG took his legs out from under him and stopped his heart from beating. He did not know if Roger Mason, Rufus Turner and Charles Shepherd were moving east or west when they were ambushed, but he thought he saw their faces streaked with light as they shot past him, their souls separated from their charred bodies in an instant.

He looked back to Hirsch's list. It read: move wall.

The sanctuary was lined with windows, but a thin beige screen ran along the back of the sanctuary. Jimmy found a latch holding the screen in place, and discovered, to his surprise that, when pushed, the screen folded up like an accordion into a hidden door at the end of a long track that ran along the floor. The sanctuary, now open, had tripled in size. He began setting up the folding chairs in long rows that rippled out in concentric half-circles from the bright light of the sanctuary to the lobby, which was covered in pale shadow.

Centcom's idea had been to locate enemy positions by drawing insurgent fire using human-shaped targets attached to the end of wooden pickets; a Marine would hide behind a wall or embankment, raise the target and *boom*, the enemy's position was clear. But the Marines soon found themselves pinned down in their positions. They decided to advance in the open, down the center of the main thoroughfare, drawing fire from the insurgents so that the rebels could be flushed out, encircled and terminated.

In Fallujah, the insurgents had taken refuge in a mosque, and Jimmy remembered the black smoke and heavy sun as he squatted, fired, and darted forwards, repeating the steps again and again. In the crackling air, he heard small arms fire whistle past him and the sound of chanting from the minarets; the voices seemed to come from everywhere at once, chanting as one, overlapping, separating and returning to the same place in a hypnotic cycle.

"What are they saying?" Jimmy asked his friends.

"What?" Charles Shepherd and Roger Mason inched closer.

The four men were close enough to one another that if they reached their arms out, they could've touched.

"Those are prayers, right?" Jimmy said.

"Yeah. What are they moaning about?" Rufus Turner shouted, as he squatted to fire on Jimmy's left.

"God is great," Charles Shepherd laughed.

"Our God or theirs?" Roger Mason said. And that was when they were hit by an RPG and Jimmy was opened up and filled with light.

Sometime before noon the choir arrived to practice, filing in one by one and taking their places to the side of the stage. They sang choral arrangements in a language Jimmy did not understand. But he did know that they, too, were singing about God.

The podium was made of solid blond oak with dark ripples of wood grain running vertically up and down its face and sides. Jimmy opened the bottle of Murphy's and poured some onto a rag. He began at the podium's left side, mechanically following the grain from top to bottom. As the wood's natural luster began to glow, Jimmy noticed that in the grain were shapes he had not at first seen. One series of ripples looked to Jimmy like the boot that was Cape Cod, another zigzagged wildly like a lightning bolt. Jimmy ran his fingers along the shapes like the newly blind students of Braille at Walter Reed Hospital. The front of the podium was adorned with a raised star that was really an inverted triangle laid over another triangle. Jimmy was careful to polish along the edges and inside the star, so that it shone as brightly as the rest of the wood. Beside the star, to the right, the grain rippled out again and Jimmy saw something that instinctively, he knew was a miracle. He felt an effusion of light gathering within him and he reached his hand out and touched the burning image.

When Jimmy came to, he lay on a hard cot in a room that flickered with fluorescent light. Father Kerslake stood over him, a look of concern etched into his face.

"Where am I?"

"Jimmy, thank God," Father Kerslake said.

"Am I dead?" Jimmy clutched the Purple Heart to his chest. It was hot to the touch, as if it had been extracted from a flame.

"What happened, Jim?"

"I saw the Virgin Mary with the baby Jesus in her arms. And then I saw – no, felt, light, amazing light, fingers of light poking in and out of me. The same as when I died."

"Jim, you didn't die."

"My friends were killed. It was my fault."

The priest looked puzzled.

"Do you feel guilty that you survived when you could have died as well?"

"I did die."

"Jim, you're in the nurse's room in the basement of the synagogue. The EMTs already checked you out. Your heart rate is up a bit, but you're fine."

"I was resurrected," Jimmy whispered. "Back in the desert. I was given a second chance."

"That's a handsome medal," Father Kerslake said, reaching for the Purple Heart. The gold cameo of General George Washington embossed into the center of the Purple Heart was silent, Washington's profile cold, noble and stern. "Can I see it?"

"Okay," Jimmy said.

"The Military Order of the Purple Heart. You have a lot to be proud of. You've done a lot in your young life."

"She was standing right before me in long robes with head bowed. She had a shining baby in her arms. I reached out my hand to touch the Blessed Mother and—"

Jimmy burst into tears.

"You passed out. That's it. Rabbi Kaminski called me to come and get you." Father Kerslake shook his head and muttered to himself. "I rushed you back to work too soon."

Rabbi Kaminski poked his head in the door. He still carried the insistent smile on his face. "How's he doing?"

"It was the Madonna," Jimmy said.

"What?" the rabbi said.

"The Madonna. I saw her," Jimmy said. "On the front of the pulpit. Plain as day."

"This could be a big problem," Rabbi Kaminski said, examining the image on the front of the pulpit. "If this gets out, we'll be overrun."

"It does look like the Madonna," Father Kerslake said. "In fact, the longer you look at it, the clearer the image seems to become. It's like she's coming out to greet us."

"But it's nothing more than a discoloration of the wood," Rabbi Kaminski said. "It could just as easily be shaped like Bugs Bunny or Daffy Duck."

"But it's not, Josh."

"What are you saying?" Rabbi Kaminski pressed.

"I'm saying: yes, it's bizarre, yes, it's strange. But these things happen for a reason. The world is at war, the Church is in crisis, there's recession, terrorism, commercialism gone wild."

"Are you saying that you think this is some sort of message from God?"

"I'm not prepared to take a position on the apparition," Father Kerslake said.

"Listen, Michael. Tomorrow is the Jewish New Year. We'll have five hundred families here. The same goes for next week on Yom Kippur, the Day of Atonement. Can you promise me that you won't let this get out of hand?"

"And what happens after the holidays? You'll be preaching to an empty synagogue for another fifty-one weeks. This could help you out, too. The ultimate interfaith dialogue."

"This sounds like a hostile takeover."

Father Kerslake laughed. "It's nothing of the sort. I'll do what I can. But young Jimmy down there thinks he's been touched by God."

"And you?"

"Josh, you know I believe that anything that inspires reflection, thoughtfulness and devotion is a good thing. Who am I to tell Jimmy he's wrong? I gave him his First Communion when he was twelve and eulogized his parents after their car wreck."

"Michael, you know he's broken beyond repair. Promise me."

"I made my promises, Josh, long ago."

"I'll just have the pulpit painted first thing tomorrow."

"Josh, you know that there is a long and colorful history to Marian visitations. In Fátima, Portugal; Lourdes, France; in Bosnia-Herzegovina. Even at a mall in South Florida. Twenty-five thousand people filled a parking lot to catch a glimpse of the Madonna on the surface of a cinnamon bun. The people will come. Use it as you will."

"Well, they'll have to wait. Tickets for the High Holidays cost two hundred dollars a person and we're all sold out."

Rabbi Kaminski stood at the pulpit, which was draped customarily in white cloth to welcome the New Year, and looked out on his congregation as the worshippers took their seats for the evening service. He saw Maxine Musher, the divorcée, trying to quiet her three children in the third row; Sam and Judy Applebaum, who had generously donated the funds to build a new library extension; David Schapiro, the MIT professor who looked perpetually confused. He saw the Coopers, the Kaplans and the Cohens settling into their seats. He even saw Michael Simon, his best friend from grade school. Jews, Rabbi Kaminski thought. They are all Jews. And why not? It's a synagogue and it's the Jewish New Year. He had worried for nothing; he would not be over- whelmed by Christian pilgrims. Father Kerslake had seen to that. Rabbi Kaminski was sure that Jimmy respected Father Kerslake's word and would do what he was asked to do. When the High Holidays were over, Rabbi Kaminski would discreetly get rid of the pulpit and order a new one; nobody would be the wiser. The pulpit had been there since before he had arrived as a student rabbi and nobody had ever seen the Madonna in the wood grain before.

The service began and the prayers were recited, though something was unusual. It seemed to the rabbi that only two-thirds of the congregation stood when they were supposed to, while the remaining congregants remained seated, causing a disturbing asymmetry to the rising wave of bodies. And the many voices that joined as one were somehow muted, as if a collective amnesia had wiped the memorized words from the brains of a portion of the congregants. For the first time since the service began, Rabbi Kaminski focused his eyes firmly on the crowd. Smiling, blissful faces stared back, faces he had never seen before – Christian faces, he couldn't say, but the style of dress was not Jewish, not the Jewish of his congregation. They smiled and stared with anticipation at the drape-covered pulpit, as if expecting it to be yanked off in a puff of smoke, like the final act of a magic show.

"There's a Native American with a buzz cut buying up tickets for the second service from congregants at the end of the access road," Cantor Magner whispered to Rabbi Kaminski during a silent prayer.

"Says who?"

"Security. And he's a real giant."

"Have him escorted off synagogue property."

"He's not on synagogue property," Cantor Magner whispered. "What can we do?"

"Is he breaking any laws?"

"There are yellow school buses lined up along the road. He's selling the tickets to the people on the buses."

"Find out if he's making a profit. That's scalping. That's a crime," Rabbi Kaminski said in something above a whisper.

"You realize," Cantor Magner said, "if we have him arrested for scalping, we have a public-relations nightmare on our hands."

"We already have one," Rabbi Kaminski said.

After the service ended, Jimmy edged forward towards the throng gathered around the rabbi, who greeted the congregants with his back pressed firmly up against the sheet-draped pulpit. Jimmy could see that Rabbi Kaminski was sweating; his eyes darted nervously about. He was talking to a young, dark-haired woman who smiled brightly and wished that he be inscribed in the Book of Life for another year. Jimmy noticed that, for once, the rabbi's insistent smile was absent. He wore something closer to a grimace, the likes of which Jimmy had only seen on the stone faces of gargoyles projecting from rooftop gutters. Jimmy pressed closer, past a woman clinging to rosary beads, and another who was massaging a worn silver cross.

"The Lord is trying to send us a message," the woman with the rosary beads said as Jimmy squeezed past her. "Well, excuse me," she huffed. "Salvation comes to those who wait."

Jimmy was an arm's length from the rabbi when someone called out, "When will you uncover the Madonna?"

The rabbi's face turned as white as the sheet that covered the vision.

"Where is the Virgin Mary?" a tall man with limp yellow hair called out. "Show us the Blessed Mother."

Jimmy had wanted to talk to the rabbi about the beauty of the prayers, how he too believed that God was his father, his king, and how, when he recited the English transliteration to the mourner's prayer, he felt that the souls of Roger Mason, Rufus Turner and Charles Shepherd were resting easy in heaven.

But now, a melee ensued, and Jimmy found himself crushed between the yellow-haired man and a bearded man in a skullcap. The two men swatted at each other with flailing fists.

"This is a place of Jewish worship. Keep your nonsense to yourself."

The yellow-haired man knocked the skullcap from the bearded man's head and replied, "A miracle has occurred here. The Mother of God is present."

"There is no Mother of God," the man countered. He bent over to pick up his skullcap. "There is God, and there is everything else."

"Anti-Christ."

"Go to hell," the man in the skullcap responded.

A woman to Jimmy's left cried, tears streaming down her face, "The Lady will save us."

Jimmy had been called to bring these people here to find spiritual and physical healing. He knew that many were lost as he had been, and that the answer lay before them underneath the sheet. A donnybrook was clearly not what he had had in mind. Jimmy knew that he could bring an end to the fighting if only he could reach the pulpit and remove the covering.

Rabbi Kaminski pounded on the pulpit with his fist. "Will everyone please calm down. This is the Jewish New Year and this is a synagogue. This is a time for reflection and peace. Please respect our Holy Day. Now, everybody, please go to your homes or to your churches and let us celebrate our holiday in peace."

"Churches?" a congregant gasped. "We're Jewish."

A squat man beside her smiled and called out, "Yes, and the Son of God was Jewish too. Show us the Holy Mother."

Rabbi Kaminski glared at the crowd. "There is no Madonna here, no Virgin Mary. You're mistaken."

A liar, Jimmy thought. He had seen it with his own eyes. "God belongs to everyone. Remove the sheet."

Later, in his study, Rabbi Kaminski sat slumped in his desk chair. Cantor Magner offered him a glass of water; the rabbi waved it away.

"It could have been worse," Cantor Magner said. "At least nobody was hurt."

"You had to call the police. They escorted two hundred Christian pilgrims out of my synagogue. There are security guards stationed at every door. And you say it could have been worse?"

"They're gone, Josh."

"They'll be back. I know how these things work. So many people are looking for hope in this world – widows, the maimed, the barren, the luckless, the mentally ill. All looking for a significant sign to let them know that everything will be all right."

"Is that not what we do here?" Cantor Magner asked.

"Dirt on a window, a blotch of discolored carbon, mineral deposits. Yes, I believe in miracles, but I don't see divinity in this excessive neediness. With these visitations, there's always a simple scientific explanation."

"We'll have the pulpit moved tonight," Cantor Magner said.

"They're keeping vigil right outside. We'll never get the pulpit past them without causing a scene."

Faint sounds of hymns could be heard in the distance through the glass walls of the synagogue.

"What do you want to do?"

"I don't know, shut the synagogue and tell the congregation that Yom Kippur services will be held at Sacred Heart."

"That's not funny."

There was a knock at the door. Cantor Magner looked quizzically at Rabbi Kaminski and then strode to the door and opened it. It was Jimmy. He stood stiffly in the doorway, his thin lips a straight, expressionless line.

"How did you get in here?" the rabbi asked.

"I never left. I hid inside the pulpit."

"Should I call security?" Cantor Magner asked.

Rabbi Kaminski suddenly felt pity for this boy who had fought for his country in a far-off land and been seriously injured. Rabbi Kaminski had seen that haunted look before – at the geriatric homes and AIDS hospices he had visited as a student rabbi. It was a look that suggested the soul had already crossed over to the other side. Jimmy was looking in on life, rather than looking out towards death.

"Let him stay," Rabbi Kaminski said. "Jimmy, why did you do this?"

"Why did you lie?"

"I don't know what you're talking about."

"The Virgin Mother. You said she was not here. You told everyone to go home. Why?"

"Jimmy, this is a synagogue."

"A House of God." He stood with his arms crossed.

"You're looking for a church," Cantor Magner interjected. "Why don't you go to St. Augustine's or Gate of Heaven? Somewhere in Southie?"

"No," he said. "Not until you share the miracle with the rest of the world."

"And then what will happen? What will be revealed?" Rabbi Kaminski asked.

"Peace, happiness. Something. I don't know, but I know that She's good and that people need her."

Rabbi Kaminski saw a film of tears form in the boy's eyes. He needs psychiatric help, he thought.

"Tell me," Cantor Magner said, stepping close to Jimmy, who did not flinch but instead straightened his already rigid pose. Cantor Magner had broad shoulders, a large square head topped with flowing white hair, and intense, probing eyes. "Tell me. When you were inside the pulpit, the one adorned with your vision, what did you see? Would it be safe to say that you were inside the Virgin Mary? Did you hear her beating heart? Did you see her lungs fill with air? Was there bright, shining light radiating from her innards?"

"No, sir. It was dark."

"Did you spring from her womb? Is that what you're trying to say?" Cantor Magner pressed.

"That's enough, Torquemada," Rabbi Kaminski said. "The boy doesn't think he's Jesus. Do you, Jim?"

"The Madonna is holding the baby Jesus in her arms."

"All right, I'm calling Father Kerslake to come pick you up."

Cantor Magner led Jimmy down the hall and found him a cold drink. Rabbi Kaminski reached Father Kerslake on his cell phone.

"Michael, guess who's standing outside my office right now?"

"Oh, no."

Rabbi Kaminski told Father Kerslake what had happened.

The priest spoke carefully. "Josh, now that word's gotten out into the community, you will be deluged with tens of thousands of pilgrims. What we have to do is work within these parameters. Obviously, you don't want these visitors to be disrespectful of your synagogue, your traditions. But by the same note, you can be sure that there are thousands of Christians who will be very sensitive towards anything sacrilegious or disrespectful towards the Madonna."

"Do you really believe this, Michael?"

"Frankly, it doesn't matter what I believe."

"This is idol worship."

"The Holy Mother is a cornerstone of the Catholic faith."

"Not in a synagogue."

"I'm trying to mediate and find a solution we can all live with. I'm not asking you to have visitors during your services, but there must be times during the day when the sanctuary is empty."

"Is this how the archdiocese is dealing with the parish closings? Move them to Beth Elohim – the Jews won't mind, they're materialistic heathens anyway."

"Don't be so cynical, Josh."

"There's got to be another way."

"How about between the hours of 2:00 p.m. and 4:00 p.m., excluding the Sabbath and High Holidays?"

"I can hear the Orthodox rabbis now. 'At last, Reform Judaism has become an official branch of Christianity.'"

The afternoon sun shone brightly through the high prisms of Temple Beth Elohim, aiming its bright yellow light directly on the sheet-draped pulpit. Jimmy had been first in line by virtue of his discovery and he listened in silence as a *Boston Globe* reporter interviewed the woman in line behind him. There were hundreds upon hundreds of pilgrims behind her.

"I came down from Marblehead to see the Blessed Mother and to pray to her to heal my son who has leukemia."

"It's an image on the wood face of a pulpit. Do you think it will work?" the reporter asked.

"Of course it will. The Madonna has revealed herself. This is the gift from God that I have been praying for."

The synagogue doors opened not a moment after 2:00 p.m. and the crowds swept past the bored security guards, whose earpieces were jammed so deep into their ears they might have been listening to an out-of-town baseball game. Jimmy felt breathless entering the sanctuary again. The sun blazed down like a spotlight, and his heart beat with anticipation for the sheet to be removed. Hirsch, the regular maintenance man, had returned from New York and was standing on the dais. He rolled his eyes and said, in an ironic tone, "Enjoy," then yanked the sheet off in a spray of dust motes that swarmed momentarily in the white light.

"It's her," the woman beside Jimmy called. "It's the Virgin Mary." She dropped to her knees and made the sign of the cross with her trembling hand.

The image was clear before Jimmy, the sun's rays seeming to penetrate deep into the wood, illuminating its golden grain from the inside. He saw how the darker grain jutted up and rounded at the top and sunk down and rounded again. He saw the impossible intricacy of its design and followed the contours with his eyes, and then he touched the image with his fingertips. It was cool to the touch, much like a high-school desktop or the lid of a coffin. The woman beside Jimmy muttered in Latin as tears poured down her face, and a man laid a bouquet of flowers at the foot of the pulpit.

Jimmy was overwhelmed by an incredible sadness as the crowd reverentially passed by and touched the wood, each person offering up a short prayer before moving on. He was overcome by sadness because he knew now that this was not a miracle, but a random image more closely signifying the years the old oak had been alive rather than anything of metaphysical significance. Yes, one could see a person clutching a baby if one chose to, but Jimmy also saw a baseball mitt, a leaning cactus and a somewhat deformed phallus in the jagged grain of the wood where the Madonna had seemingly revealed herself. The image reminded him of the inkblot tests that the doctors at Landstuhl Medical Center in Germany had forced him to analyze before shipping him back home.

He had been mistaken.

Nobody else seemed to notice. The supplicants continued to pass by, placing their hands on the image, offering prayers and leaving money, flowers and tokens of their faith before the pulpit. The woman who had been beside Jimmy began wailing as a thin man wearing a priest's collar softly asked her to move on so that others could also pray before the Mother.

"My baby, my baby," she cried. "Save my baby."

But Jimmy knew that the boy with leukemia would not be saved. He would disappear from the earth like Jimmy's friends, Roger Mason, Rufus Turner and Charles Shepherd, leaving an impossible void that even the most earnest prayer would never fill.

Jimmy searched the sanctuary and spotted the rabbi, who stood at a distance, beside the man who had interrogated Jimmy in the rabbi's study. Rabbi Kaminski looked on, as a man carrying a large wooden cross knelt before the image. Jimmy was no more than ten steps away when he caught the rabbi's eye. Jimmy nodded, and the rabbi spun on his heels and disappeared around a corner.

Jimmy had to apologize. He had wanted something else that now seemed unimaginable – not this farce. The Madonna had not revealed herself at all. He searched the back halls that housed classrooms and offices, and knocked on the rabbi's study door. But, it seemed that Rabbi Kaminski was trying to avoid Jimmy with the same vigor that Jimmy was trying to find him.

Jimmy returned the next day, and the day after that. Each time there were more pilgrims camped out along the tree-lined path that led to the main road, and each time the rabbi blanched at the sight of him and disappeared. On the fourth day, as Jimmy searched among the worshippers who chanted as they waited for their meeting with the false Madonna, he was confronted by the square-jawed man with the flowing white hair. He stopped Jimmy with an outstretched arm.

"What you are looking for is over there," he said, and pointed to the pulpit. "There's nothing else here for you."

"I want to speak to the rabbi," Jimmy said.

"The rabbi is not available," Cantor Magner said.

"It was a mistake. I didn't mean to—"

"You didn't mean to what?"

"There are – no Jews here."

"It's two days before Yom Kippur, the holiest day of the year for Jews. They're praying in the middle school gymnasium down the street. So you and your missionaries will have to talk amongst yourselves."

"No, you're mistaken. I need to speak to the rabbi," Jimmy pleaded. "To apologize."

"The rabbi does not take confession," Cantor Magner said, and stalked away in his dark blue suit.

Rabbi Kaminski overheard and felt that if Jimmy needed to speak to him that badly he could refuse him no longer. "What do you think an apology does for my congregation right now? Yom Kippur is in two days."

Jimmy was silent and then said, "I don't know what to say. What can I do?"

Rabbi Kaminski said, "You need to make this right somehow."

Jimmy was being chased by the dead: Roger Mason, Rufus Turner, Charles Shepherd, his mother, his father, the boy with leukemia, the dozens of nameless Iraqis he had seen crumpled at the side of the road during his tour of duty. All of them followed Jimmy, their bodies persisting in the ravaged state of their deaths. Jimmy's father had been impaled by the steering column of his Buick Century; Charles Shepherd's jaw had been blown off; an Iraqi outside the city of Ramadi was so badly decomposed that his bright bones showed through. Each of these specters chased him, bearing aloft a giant wooden cross that Jimmy knew was meant for him.

He woke in the darkness with a gasp, felt the weight of something heavy on his chest, and threw his Purple Heart clattering into the corner.

"Be careful with that," a voice said. "That's a Sacred Heart."

"What? Who's there?"

"That's a Purple Heart." It was John Fishercat. "They're earned with blood."

Jimmy's eyes acclimatized to the murky gray light. It was dusk and he heard boys playing outside on the street.

John Fishercat turned on Jimmy's bedside lamp and sat on the end of the bed. He popped a can of beer and offered one to Jimmy, who shook it away. "Bad dreams?"

"What have I done?" Jimmy said. "Just ripples in the wood. I thought I was doing good. I thought I was helping people, but I just made a mess of everything."

"Jimmy, I wasn't going to question what you believe. The Great Spirit wears many costumes."

"But God," Jimmy said. "Nobody owns God."

"No," John Fishercat said. "Nobody does. The Great Spirit is everywhere."

"I wanted to make people happy, bring them comfort, but now, that synagogue—"

"It's a circus act," John Fishercat interjected.

"I've caused more harm than good," Jimmy said. "Remember how you used to talk about the Great Spirit and how he watches over everyone? Up there on the roof, under that big sky, I felt like I was so close to that spirit. When I'm up there, I can see everything. But down here, it's confusing."

John Fishercat stood up to his full height. With Jimmy still lying supine on the bed, the master roofer looked like a giant. "Jimmy, you're the best roofer I've ever known. You belong up there, not down here. We can fix this problem. Now get out of bed," he said, extending his massive hand. "We have work to do."

"Work?" Jimmy said. He felt a wave of nerves ripple through his stomach. "But, what about the insurance?"

"Forget the insurance," John Fishercat, said smiling. "This is an act of God."

The morning sun was beginning to rise in the east, and in the growing light, Jimmy could see that down below a makeshift tent city had sprung up in the woods around the synagogue. Police cars sat on the sidewalk, blocking the entrance. He gazed at the Charles River with its snaking route back to the Atlantic, the pointed church steeples that dotted the landscape as far as the eye could see. Jimmy and John Fishercat had scaled the sheer glass walls of the temple under the cover of darkness and now they stood perched near the very apex of the glass structure. The climb had been difficult, aided only by large rubber suctions and John Fishercat's words of encouragement. But, as he leaned against the glass panel and breathed in the cool, piney late-September air, Jimmy felt as if he had returned home at last. John Fishercat was confident that they would be able to extract the pulpit without too much difficulty. He had once lowered a baby grand piano through a gap he had cut in the roof of a state senator's mansion, though he had used a crane to assist him. The pulpit, however, was not that heavy. John Fishercat told Jimmy he could lift it with one hand tied behind his back.

John Fishercat lay back with his eyes closed, a broad grin on his face. In the silence just before the sun breached the horizon, Jimmy heard the very gears of the world turning. Everything that had been so confusing suddenly seemed clear: he had not killed his friends. They had not died because they were facing west rather than east and they had not died because they were standing too close to answer Jimmy's questions about the Muslim prayers. They had died in a war they did not control. In fact, Jimmy knew that down on the ground, he didn't control anything at all – nobody did. But up high, with the cool breeze caressing his face and the sun coming up to meet him, he felt that he could live forever.

"Ready?" John Fishercat asked, as he slowly slid down along the glass.

Jimmy took a deep breath and looked through the glass panel: the pulpit stood directly beneath them in the gray darkness.

"Okay," Jimmy said.

Despite the steep pitch of the roof, removing the glass panels was no more difficult than popping out a fixed skylight; the windows were square here and easier to remove than the pointed triangles up above. Jimmy and John Fishercat balanced themselves on the corrugated metal frame beneath the window, cut open the caulking with their utility knives and pulled back the waterproof sealant with their hands. Jimmy could now see that the laminated glass panes that had cast such brilliant light onto the pulpit down below were actually comprised of two pieces of glass sandwiching a piece of plastic, which rendered the glass shatterproof. They removed four panels and placed them into the knapsack on John Fishercat's back.

He removed a thick rope from his belt and dropped one end down into the sanctuary. "All right, Jim."

John Fishercat's arms were as thick and strong as the gnarled roots of an old tree. Jimmy climbed onto the rope and floated in the air for a moment.

"I want to thank you for helping me make this right."

"Don't forget your tools," John Fishercat said. "You can bet somebody has nailed it down."

Because of the crowds waiting outside, the doors to the synagogue had opened earlier and earlier each morning – and had stayed open for visitation later and later each night. Rabbi Kaminski had not yet given word that the *Kol Nidre* service at the synagogue would be canceled. Services at the nearby middle school gym had been sparsely attended, and the thought of presiding over such a small crowd on the eve of Yom Kippur depressed him to no end.

Is this how the Jews have survived all these thousands of years? General indifference? It would not have been that way in his grandfather's generation, he thought sadly. But the world had changed. So many of

his congregants only showed up twice a year, at Rosh
Hashanah and Yom Kippur. Soon, they wouldn't show
up at all. What was it that excited the Christians so
much? Was it the recognizable characters who seemingly held super powers in their hands, who asked for little and returned Salvation? The Father, the Son and the
Holy Ghost. Which one was supposed to be God? And
where did the Madonna fit into this triptych?

Rabbi Kaminski had taken to sleeping, fully dressed,
in his office, in case anything got out of hand at the synagogue. Who was he kidding? Everything had gotten out
of hand, and it was his fault. His synagogue had been
hijacked, but the only alternative would have been a holy
war, and that was no alternative at all.

He rinsed out his mouth in the water fountain and
stepped sleepily down the hall, clipping his *kippa* to his
mussed hair. He heard the crowds clamoring outside the
main door, and an officious policeman enunciating
through a megaphone: "Please line up in single file.
Single file only to see the Madonna."

Rabbi Kaminski heard the doors unlatch, and the
scurry of rushing feet across the tiles of the lobby. He
opened the hall door leading into the sanctuary.

The pulpit was gone.

His wish had come true. It had simply disappeared
overnight.

The crowd gasped as one, and Rabbi Kaminski felt
in his gut a warm boyish satisfaction that he had not felt
in years.

"Look," someone called from the crowd. "The Madonna, she's floating up to heaven."

Many among the crowd fell to their knees and crossed themselves.

"Now, this is a genuine miracle," a man in front of Rabbi Kaminski said. "Another gift from God."

Rabbi Kaminski raised his head and saw his former pulpit, bound by a thick rope, rising higher and higher into the bright morning light, the image on the front, abstract as it was, burning brightly. As the pulpit neared the apex of the sanctuary, pilgrims began to cry out for the Blessed Mother: "We'll wait until you return. We'll pray until we're worthy of you."

The pilgrims were too caught up with the image on the front of the pulpit to notice that anyone was hiding inside, but Rabbi Kaminski saw Jimmy's face peer over the lip of the pulpit. Even if they had seen Jimmy, Rabbi Kaminski figured, they likely would have thought he was an angel assisting the Holy Mother on her journey, barbed as he was with a crown of bright morning sunlight. Jimmy caught the rabbi's eye and offered a relieved smile.

But Rabbi Kaminski could not smile back, as he was now the caretaker of the newest shrine in all of Christendom and he still had Yom Kippur to attend to.

What Is It Then, Between Us?

Hightower lay naked in the cold darkness waiting for Jenny to return from the bathroom. The heat was out again and he stroked himself absently beneath the sheets, listening for the radiator to rattle and kick on. Ever since she had taken it from behind on a pile of coats at a Christmas party in Canarsie years back, Hightower knew she was all he would ever want. At one time or another, he had done Jenny upside down and backwards and everywhere in between: he'd gone down on her on the F train and flicked his tongue so she'd come as the train burst out of the tunnel and shot past distant, doll-like Lady Liberty, he'd spanked her with the sole of his shoe and she'd cried out for more, he'd even fucked her in the ass dozens of times and she had bucked against him, saying "Harder, Vinny, harder."

But now, her ass was off limits and she had scolded him last month when he had come in her mouth. "You wanna get me pregnant or not?" she'd said.

Hightower couldn't figure out her cycle and he was forced to find relief in Jenny's perfumed lotions, gels and creams, mixed with his own spit to find the slickest glide.

"What are you doing?" Jenny stood in the doorway wearing the sickly snot-colored bathrobe that Hightower had been threatening to throw down the air shaft.

"I'm getting ready for you."

"It looks like you're finished," she said, tossing him some wrinkled tissues she dug from her bathrobe pocket.

"Oh, yeah? I can go again."

"Forget it," she said. "I'm not ovulating."

Everything was about her uterus and her tubes and her ovaries and other things he'd never heard of before. He'd thought an embryo sounded like some sort of burrito and that the birth canal was where Moses had been born in the reeds. Hightower wasn't used to fucking on a schedule. He felt like he was failing science class again because he couldn't understand why you couldn't make a baby any day of the month. When she gave him the cold shoulder, he felt his prick would fall off like rotten fruit from a branch.

"There's no heat," Jenny said. Her dyed blonde hair looked green in the dull light of the hallway.

"We can make our own," he responded, flexing his abs so his penis reared up momentarily.

"Enough. All right, Vincent? I'm crampy, I'm tired and I'm freezing."

He climbed out of bed and began to get dressed.

"Where are you going?" she asked.

"To get the boiler fixed."

Jenny stood before Hightower, her arms crossed. She looked to him like the schoolteacher she was, her big glasses perched on her thin nose, her shoulders straight. Hightower pulled a sweater over his head and stared at her for a long, empty moment.

"What is it then?" she said. "You want your wife to go out in the cold?"

He leaned in to kiss her.

"Not my lips."

They were coated with some sort of glossy medicinal salve that smelled to Hightower of gym class and sweat socks.

"I don't care," he said, leaning in again.

"But I do. Okay?"

He kissed her throat and down her neck towards her breasts. He felt a vein jump and thought he heard Jenny gasp the way she did before losing herself, but it was a long, exasperated, frowning sigh.

"Vincent. Find Cliff and get the heat turned back on."

"Well, I'm turned back on," he said, trying to ignite a spark.

"Please," she whispered plaintively. "What if we had a child freezing to death in here?"

Her blue eyes were watery and cold, reflecting in them that loathsome, needy creature that Hightower became when he couldn't get close enough to Jenny. He'd already gotten rid of his bench press and weights to make room for a hand-me-down crib and changing table from Jenny's fat, older sister. There was no child and already Jenny was taking its side like it owned a piece of her. He got a handful of her hair in his hand and pulled her close; her heart beat between them.

"Don't," she said.

"Don't yourself," he said, and kissed her hard on the mouth.

Cliff was their alcoholic super who lived in a basement apartment two blocks over. His phone was usually dead, and sometimes he had the shakes so bad he couldn't screw in a lightbulb, but he was the only person east of the Hudson with a key to the basement and the furnace. His barred window was dark, but staggered footprints in the dirty snow pointed Hightower in the right direction.

Jackie's Fifth Amendment was the local dump where Hightower had learned to drink. As a schoolkid he'd watched his father kill afternoons there. Later, he had taken Jenny to Jackie's when he and Jenny first started going together. But he hadn't been to Jackie's in a long time, not since he'd gotten out of jail and started hauling crates for a local soda company.

"Turn over a new leaf," Jenny had said optimistically. That was when she started yakking about babies, and Hightower figured he'd better make like a husband or else.

The long, low-ceilinged bar was jammed with laughing young men and women, many of whom had recently crossed the East River to escape Manhattan's runaway rents. The bar was interspersed here and there with the hardened faces of old-timers, fixtures at Jackie's as long as Hightower could remember. He saw his next door neighbors, Hank and Cele Polniaszeki, squeezed together at a small banquette near the salt-streaked picture window, drinking orange highballs that glowed in the half-darkness. He saw Elvis Doyle stumble from the bathroom zipping his fly, and the panhandling black from the ATM on Ninth Street counting coins in his gloved hands. Cliff was usually perched on a stool before the lone television that hung above the cash register, his face dipping to meet the edge of his glass. But now a group of young women crowded the bar, waving folded bills in the air. Their asses looked like big fat hearts and Hightower wanted to crush himself into them. Some were pretty and some weren't, but they all smelled of perfume and sweat and cigarettes and something reckless that Hightower had been missing in Jenny since she'd gotten it in her head to get knocked up.

He pressed himself up to the bar and ordered a Maker's Mark on the rocks.

"Look what the cat dragged in," Jackie said, laughing until he was overcome by a dry, heaving cough. "How's jail?"

"Been out awhile," Hightower said.

"I mean the marital prison," Jackie said. "You're only free when you're dead."

"Come off it," Hightower said. "You seen Cliff?"

"I told him to take his DTs and hit the road. He hasn't paid his tab in over a year. What do you want with that deadbeat, anyway?"

"Oil burner's on the fritz and Jenny's on the war-path."

Jackie winked and laughed. "You know what I'd do to warm her up?"

"Beats me," Hightower said.

Jackie made a crude pushing motion with his closed fist. "Nice and easy," he added, slapping his palm on the bar for emphasis.

"Are you talking about fucking my wife? Is that it?" Hightower said. He felt like reaching across the bar and pummeling Jackie in his ashcan face. "You thinking about fucking the mother of my child?"

"Vinny, relax. I was joking around. I had no idea."

"You can say that again." Hightower straightened up and added, "I'm going to be a father."

"Well, congrats," Jackie said, sliding the drink towards Hightower. "This one's on the house."

Hightower raised the glass and downed the bourbon in one burning gulp.

Jackie smiled and poured another. "Believe me, Vin. I couldn't be happier." He slid the second drink forward. "Couldn't be happier."

The jukebox played a sad song that Hightower recognized but could not place. The bar was full and there was nowhere to sit. Hank and Cele were arguing again and Elvis paced back and forth in front of the two rotary pay phones, waiting for one of them to ring. Through the picture window, Hightower could see a *Daily News* truck skidding through the falling snow, the flickering red and orange lights of the adjacent bodega blinking on and off. Long, jagged icicles hung from the frayed awning outside. He caught a glimpse of himself in the mirror behind the bar and saw that his chest was broad and muscular, that his face was still handsome and that nobody could say no to Vincent Hightower.

He heard laughing at the table behind him and saw that the four women with the valentine asses were toasting something with a dramatic clink of their glasses. Hightower slid his wedding band from his finger and dropped it into his jeans pocket.

He squeezed in beside a redhead whose hair was styled in a severe bob. She wore a tight, low-cut sweater and Hightower couldn't help but think that her freckled white skin was waiting to flush red under him. "What are you celebrating?"

"And who are you?" the redhead said flatly.

"Oh, come on," one of the other girls said. "Be nice."

"I'm Vinny," he said, extending his hand.

"That's too perfect," the redhead said, turning back to her drink and laughing a dry laugh.

"What's the matter? I'm making nice," Hightower said.

"And I'm sure that's your real name," the redhead said.

"I'm Antoinette," one of the girls across the table said. She had a full, round face and ringlets that fell past her shoulders. "This is Jasmine, Emma and—"

"Stella," the redhead interrupted.

"Stella?" one of the girls asked. Her face was already a drunken smear.

"Yeah," the redhead said. "That's right."

"Well, nice to meet you, Stella." Hightower extended his hand. "What are you celebrating?"

"Antoinette and Emma are moving to Brooklyn," Stella said, sucking on a lime rind.

"The Slope," one of the others added with a knowing nod of her head.

What she could do with that mouth, Hightower thought. "Hey, Brooklyn's more better than Manhattan. You've got the Cyclone and Coney Island—"

"More better. Did you hear that?" Stella shrieked.

She turned back to Hightower. "You're the real thing."

"That's the God's honest truth," Hightower said.

"Do you say 'dem' and 'dose' and 'dat' as well or is that just in the movies?"

"I'll say whatever you want me to say," Hightower said.

"Sure," Stella said. "But first, buy us another round."

"Come with me," he responded.

Stella just shook her head slowly and crunched an ice cube between her teeth.

"I'll go," Antoinette said.

Antoinette was short and pear-shaped with the shining, pocked complexion of a new golf ball. She reminded Hightower of those Catholic schoolgirls up the street at Saint Saviour who walked with their twisting hips, confident that what they had under their skirts was more valuable than gold.

"Do you live around here?" she asked. Her brow wrinkled when she posed the question and Hightower realized that she was the dog of the group.

"Yeah," Hightower said. "Grew up here."

"I'm from upstate, near Syracuse," she said. "I got my MFA from Sarah Lawrence in the spring and now I'm sort of working." She ordered four glasses of Beaujolais. And then: "Okay, whatever your house red is."

Hightower looked back to the table and saw Stella craning her long neck so the lean cords stood out against her skin. Antoinette asked Hightower what he wanted.

"I want to fuck your friend," he whispered in her double-pierced ear.

"What about me?" she said, her large brown eyes wide, unblinking.

Her breasts were big enough, Hightower thought, but she had a slight paunch. "Are you pregnant?" he asked.

"I'm on the pill," she whispered. "You could fuck me all night."

"What about her?" Hightower said, tossing his head in Stella's direction. He felt Antoinette's hand on his thigh.

"She's no good." She pulled Hightower's face down to her height and bit him hard on the lip.

Lately, Hightower was used to being the pursuer. It had been a long time since Jenny had initiated anything with him, since he'd woken with his hard cock in her mouth, crying out for Jesus, and he couldn't remember the last time she sat astride his hips thrusting him deep inside her. Now, she lay on her back with a distracted look on her face that made Hightower want to slap her silly. She counted down time as his cum dripped inside her, a pillow jammed beneath her ass.

Hightower and Antoinette took their seats at the table. His lip stung where she had bit him. He felt himself stiffen. Stella took her drink, and, without thanking Hightower, clinked glasses with the others.

"But seriously, the only thing people want to read these days is clever irony, and this lack of gravitas pisses me off. Sometimes a manuscript comes in that I know is deep and moving, but my instinct tells me that nobody's going to look at it because it doesn't fit the template of what people are reading these days." Stella put her drink down and shook her head. "I feel like a cigarette."

"I'll smoke with you," Hightower said, indicating the entry vestibule.

Stella eyed the window. Outside, beneath the awning, a couple of regulars stood hunched, puffing damp cigarettes against the blowing snow. "I'm not a fucking addict, okay? I can control myself."

Emma laughed and Antoinette rolled her eyes.

"I was just trying to be nice."

"Well, don't. I don't need your kindness."

"I should let you know," Antoinette said, "she's permanently on the rag."

"Fuck you," Stella said.

"I'm only joking," Antoinette said.

"So, what are you, some kind of writer?" He could feel the heat from her thighs moving from her body to his, and he felt that irrational ache inside that said if he didn't fuck her, he would die.

"I'm an editor." She turned to face him for the first time. "Do you read?"

"You bet I read."

"What do you read?" She tapped her short finger-nails on the table.

"What, are you kidding? I read books."

"Name one," she said. Her eyes were hard and her thin lips were bright and unmoving like a slash of blood. "And it can't be a movie as well."

"Ignore her," Antoinette said.

All the blood in his body flowed to his cock, but the words he had long ago learned in school appeared in his mind. "'The woods are lovely, dark, and deep / But I have promises to keep / And miles to go before I sleep / And miles to go before I sleep.'"

"Bravo," Antoinette said, clapping her hands. She smiled at Hightower. "That's good."

"'Stopping by Woods on a Snowy Evening.' Frost." Stella said. "Do you know what that means?"

"Do you?" Hightower said.

"Who else do you read?" Stella said.

Hightower remembered that there were words etched into the low fence at the Fulton Ferry Landing where Jenny had taken him once to watch the sunset. The smell of the briny water had made him think that Jenny was wet and he'd slid his hand into her pants to find that she was. "That one about the Brooklyn Ferry."

"Whitman?" she said, exasperated. "Don't you read anyone who's not a dead white male? Have you ever read Toni Morrison, or Jhumpa Lahiri, or Edwidge Danticat?"

"None of your goddamn business if I read any of those guys."

Hightower realized with stark gut-twisting finality that the old Brooklyn he had grown up in was changing in a way he did not recognize. He'd seen it coming for years and had cracked jokes as the moving vans came and went, but had never imagined a complete takeover. There was a time when kids on his block would laugh at you if you read a book, call you 'perfessor' and kick you in the balls. Now, bodegas were being turned into boutiques and bistros all up and down Fifth Avenue, nearly all the way to Sunset Park. A bar was where you went to get drunk. Jackie had poured generously, assuring a cheap buzz for his neighborhood friends. The cigarette smoke had been so thick and cancerous it would choke you. Now, you had to take your smokes outside in the rain and snow, like a common criminal.

"Enough with this elitist crap," Antoinette said.

"It's not elitist. It's the truth. I'll bet I can tell you in fifty words or less your entire pathetic biography."

Hightower gulped down the rest of his drink, wiped his mouth, and glared at Stella. "Give it your best shot."

Jasmine and Emma seemed to be paying attention to Hightower for the first time, their eyes locked on his sweating face.

"You grew up within three blocks of here, live in the same building your alcoholic parents lived, or still live. You've never left the city, never seen the world . . ." She paused. "Unless you were in the service, or in jail. You think you need a passport to go to Manhattan and you don't cross the bridges more than three times a year. You're a high-school dropout and you're single. You'll die penniless, never knowing the first thing about life, and you'll be buried in Queens and forgotten, mourned by no one."

She stared at him hard, her eyes unblinking. "Truth hurts, doesn't it?"

"Ouch," Jasmine said.

Hightower did not smile, but sullenly retorted, "Those tits of yours are fakes. I've seen better cans in the dog food aisle at C-Town."

"I'm going out for a cigarette," Stella said, pushing past Hightower. "*Don't* come with me."

Jasmine and Emma joined her, wrapping thick wool scarves around their pale necks.

Hightower was left alone at the table with Antoinette, who smiled softly. "Don't mind Jane. She's got issues."

"Jane?"

"She's really Jane Templeton from Bethesda, Maryland. She likes to play the bitch. It makes her feel powerful when she's away from Daddy's money."

Hightower noticed that the crowds were thinning out and that Hank and Cele had left their spot by the window. The jukebox played an old Louis Prima song about love.

"Why you so nice?"

"I don't know," Antoinette said. "I like you."

By the way her voice wavered, Hightower could tell that she was used to picking up the leftovers. She looked so pathetic that he wanted to fuck her hard, so it hurt, teach her not to be kind to strangers. What did she know about him, anyway? He didn't need her pity.

He stood up and his thighs lifted the table, nearly knocking over the wine glasses. "I've got to piss."

Hightower slammed the bathroom door behind him, and seconds later Antoinette appeared in the tiny cubicle. A single bare bulb swung on a cord above them. The stamped tin walls were flaked with rust, and the smell of fifty years of urine burned in his nose.

"What do you want?" He saw her warped blue-green reflection in the buffed metal slab that served as a mirror.

"This," she said, reaching for his buckle. She sat on the toilet seat and undid his belt. Behind him, a hulking radiator hissed and sizzled. She unzipped him and fished inside his pants. "You're big," she said. "It's all right, honey. I know what I'm doing."

He wanted to piss in her face, show her that he was in charge, but he was too hard to do anything other than lean back and close his eyes. He could hear her breathing slowly as she bent to take him in her mouth, and then the suction of her lips sliding around him. The radiator steamed and sizzled against his bare ass, the water bubbling up from the furnace below. He could feel his own quivering intake of breath as he leaned back against the boiling heater, his blood rushing through his veins, both pain and pleasure mixed as one. Antoinette cupped her hands around his ass and eased him away from the burning heater.

He looked down and saw that with her ringlets of hair spread out against her broad back Antoinette looked like a buffalo at feed. She was sucking with greater urgency now, her head moving in a brutal rhythm. But he couldn't stop her, his muscles as soft and warm as chewed bubblegum, and when he tried to pull away, he could feel her teeth scraping lightly against his shaft. And then he came, in her mouth, across her lips and in the stray ringlets of her hair. Her round face rose to meet his.

"So, we're going to be neighbors," she said. "We can make this regular."

"I gotta go," he said, pulling up his pants.

"What do you mean? I just gave you head."

"You want a fucking medal?"

"No, it's just—" She still had cum in the corner of her mouth, and in the meager light of the bathroom he saw a child with vanilla ice cream on her lips.

"It's just nothing. That's it. A big nothing." He zipped his pants and swung out of the bathroom.

He was too upset to even insult Stella on the way out, and he burst into the cold night wanting Jenny more than he had ever wanted her before. The clouds above seemed to be lit from within, as if all of those who had died and those yet to be born were casting their frozen ashes onto his head. He made his block in a minute flat and a minute later, he stood at the door of his apartment.

The stairs had never looked so daunting before, even when he had hauled a sofa up on his back. He stood in the dim foyer, his heart thumping in his chest, and then took the stairs two at a time. Jenny was still up, doing a crossword in bed.

"Vin? That you?"

He could hear the radiator banging and rattling, steam sizzling from the spigot.

"Yeah. It's me."

Jenny appeared in the doorway in an oversized pajama top, her hair tied back in a ponytail. "The heat," she said sheepishly. "It came on by itself right after you left. I called out for you but you didn't hear."

"That's okay," he said. "As long as we have heat now."

He felt relieved at the sight of her and he started to speak.

"Baby," she said. "I'm sorry for being like that before, making you go out into the snow for nothing. Come here."

He moved forward, but slowly.

"You been drinking?"

"I take the Fifth."

"How many?" she smiled.

"A couple."

She laughed. "It's stupid, I know, but when you didn't come back I thought maybe something happened to you, you got beat up or something. And then I thought, 'My man, he's strong, he can take care of himself.' And I got really horny waiting for you, and I felt we could do it like old times, however you want, or just plain old-fashioned fucking. What do you think?"

"Isn't it a school night?" A cold drop of semen dripped down his pant leg.

"Don't be that way, Vinny. I know I've had babies on the brain and haven't been the best lover, but, let's fuck," she said, pulling him towards the bed. Her hands were soft and warm.

"No," Hightower said. "Not tonight."

"Come on, baby. I know I sent you out in the cold, but I apologized. Don't make me beg for it."

Hightower saw in Jenny that desperation he had been feeling all those months, when he couldn't get close enough to her.

"I'm not going to fuck you," he said raffishly. "But I'll help you out."

He tossed her onto the bed, pulled off her pajama shirt and yanked off her cotton panties. Then he buried his face between her legs until he was swallowed by darkness.

A Kiss for Mrs. Fisch

Gesh still had his mother's pink lipstick on his cheek when the packed 747 took off from Kennedy Airport. As the plane left the earth, Gesh realized that he had never felt so alone. So, this is what it's like to be an orphan, Gesh thought. He could still hear his father's words: "My son the millionaire is not ready to retire. It's time to stop babying him. Say a prayer. He's gone."

What kind of fortieth birthday present was this? An airplane ticket and out on the curb. They had talked about it for months, but Gesh hadn't believed that his parents would really pack up and move to Florida. His mother complained about the mosquitoes and the humidity. His father thought the Jews down there were boorish and low class. But, all their friends had already made the move, so it was only natural that they follow. Now, retirement, and shut out of the business. Weinstock Industrial Kitcheners on the Bowery sold to a China-man. Gesh couldn't run a lemonade stand, his father had said. But Gesh would be taken care of through a trust fund. His cousin Marty, the schmuck, would keep an eye on him. What a life.

"Maybe you'll marry a nice Jewish girl," his mother had said.

On the airplane, Gesh read magazines his mother had packed, and later drank some tea that the pretty stewardess brought for him. He had tragically attempted to flirt with her by saying, "How about some honey, honey," when she'd asked if he wanted sugar or cream. Later, she laid a blanket over his drowsing body, and as he drifted into sleep he thought of Israel, that magical Land of Milk and Honey from his Hebrew school days. He dreamt about Adam in the Garden of Eden, and his wife God made out of Adam's own rib; he dreamt about Abraham, who had a child at the age of ninety, and King Solomon the Wise who had more than one hundred wives. A sunny land of miracles where anything was possible.

It was a bright, sunny October day when Marty and his wife Debbie picked Gesh up at Ben Gurion airport. Marty had married Debbie nearly two years ago, a busty blonde with frizzy shoulder-length hair, a long narrow face and sparkling blue eyes. Gesh had met her once at a Passover Seder in New York and she had asked Gesh questions about himself, and actually waited for his response. Gesh liked her and wanted to say, "Ain't you too good for this *schlub*?" But, he kept his mouth shut.

Marty hugged Gesh and helped him throw his bags into the trunk. "You haven't aged a bit, kid. But get a shave, why don't you. You look like a goddamn Cossack." Marty ran his fingers through his own graying beard. "How's the old leg?"

Marty was two-and-a-half months younger than Gesh, and was the only son of Gesh's Aunt Phyllis. He was the closest thing Gesh had to a brother. Gesh thought his cousin Marty was a windbag and a hypocrite, who had, himself, lived with his mother until three years earlier, when the Angel of Death had called a foul on her for too many cigarettes. Marty hadn't given a shit about Israel before he moved, but now he talked as if he had lived there for five thousand years.

"Welcome home," Marty smiled. "Your exile is over at last."

Gesh stayed in his new room for three days, lying on the bed, staring at the ceiling. The few times he emerged to relieve himself, he quickly returned, head down to avoid seeing his reflection in the hallway mirror — the thinning weed-like hair; the high, sloping forehead, rounded like the butt-end of a melon; the eyebrows, thick and black like road-killed caterpillars; the comical sweet potato nose; the lumpy pink lips that seemed to smile upside down whenever his mouth opened to mix up words. At six-foot-four, Gesh was nearly a foot taller than Marty. The bed was too short for him. His stocking feet hung off the end of the mattress like limp puppets. The tap water tasted funny, of rusted metal and something worse, but he refused the bottled water that was offered to him, thinking, God forbid I ever get that fancy.

He had lived with his parents for the entire forty years of his life, except for two weeks at sleep-away camp when he was twelve. He never imagined a time when they would not be there. Even at summer camp, his mother wrote him every day, asking after his leg. His mother was the first person he saw every morning, and the last person he saw every night.

Gesh felt a pang of loss for the life he had had in New York City. He'd been happy. It had been a simple life; he had nothing to complain about. He knew where the good movie theatres were so that he could sit in the dark all day and watch people's lives unfold without being seen. He knew where to grab coffee and the *Daily News* for under a dollar, and where not to walk after dark. But here, in Jerusalem, he was afraid if he looked the wrong way and stepped off the curb he could be wiped out with a car up his ass before he knew what hit him. And the language. What kind of crazy talk was this? Years ago, Gesh had studied Hebrew for his Bar Mitzvah, but not a single word he heard at the airport – shouted, always shouted – made any sense to him. The Israelis seemed so confident, so wilful as they spoke their gibberish. Gesh could only shake his head. In New York, he knew that the cabbies driving crosstown, the delivery men down in the Bowery, even the turbaned man with the snack cart who poured Gesh's coffee outside the 6 train, would understand him even if it meant that Gesh had to speak slowly. Here, there was no hope. They would never understand him.

He even missed his father's morning ritual, his gruff voice, fist banging on the bathroom door, "What? You fall in, Gesh? Come on, I'm bursting." Gesh wondered what his parents were doing at that very moment. But he didn't even know if it was nighttime or daytime back in Florida, and he felt an empty space open up inside him.

The sun was out when Gesh awoke. His mouth tasted sour and his bladder was full. His cousin's bedroom door was open a crack. As he passed by on the way to the bathroom, Debbie's face turned away, Gesh noticed that she was flipping her hair into some kind of elastic. Her skin was soft and smooth and reminded Gesh of the little rolls he loved to eat at weddings and Bar Mitzvahs. She had a tangled dark patch of hair between her legs and stark white breasts that hung down as she bent over to pull on her panties. She had a small belly that flattened out when she straightened. She snapped the elastic of her underwear firm against her hips, and Gesh noticed that her breasts, though a nice handful, were not as large as those he had seen in magazines. She hummed quietly as she lifted a bra from her bed and put her arms through the loops. What a contraption. He thought back to the straps and cords on his long-abandoned leg brace. She seemed to be having difficulty snapping the bra closed. She fiddled with the clasp, biting her tongue in concentration. Slowly, she turned her head and noticed Gesh standing in the doorway. Her blue eyes were calm and peaceful. She drifted over to the door and pushed it closed with the delicacy of a kiss.

When Gesh spoke to his mother later that week, her voice sounded tiny, thin, lost.

"How's your leg?"

"Fine, Ma. It hasn't hurt in years."

"You're not happy?"

Gesh was silent.

"Are you there, Gesh?" his mother asked.

Then his father grabbed the phone from her. "Gershom," he said. "We want you to come to Florida."

"What?" Gesh said.

"Your mother is going to have a stroke if Marty calls one more time. He says you're moping and won't leave your room. We've been thinking," his father said, taking a deep breath. "We want you to come and stay with us again."

His father blamed himself for Gesh's polio, and needled Gesh for his weak leg. His father was convinced that it was his fault, that something must have been wrong with him for his only son to be afflicted so. He had wanted Gesh to grow up to be the next Hank Greenberg, hammering home runs for the hometown Yankees. But his son was just a lump, and a goddamn Mets fan.

"You didn't make it, kid. No big deal," his father growled. "Hey, I bought you Mets tickets for spring training at Port St. Lucie. Behind home plate. Terrific seats. What do you say?"

Gesh hung up the phone.

"You hung up on Uncle Louie?" Marty screamed, with such force Gesh thought that his cousin's hair plugs might pop out of his scalp.

"Gesh, why don't you go somewhere today?" Debbie said with a light smile. "Go for a walk."

Near Zion Square, Gesh sat on a bench outside a kiosk that announced its wares with a handwritten sign that said: BEER & MINERALS. He spent the morning watching the parade of people that passed before him – young female soldiers wearing tight olive-green pants, long-legged tourists in shorts, housewives with bags of groceries, lovers holding hands, laughing Arab girls.

A few feet away, a squat, bearded man in a worn suit was torturing a bass saxophone. It was the largest, loudest saxophone Gesh had ever seen. The man played as if his fingers had been replaced by toes. Beside the man stood his wife, with her hand on his shoulder. She was a round woman, and wore a blue dress and an aquamarine hat that sparkled with sequins. She was missing some teeth and had the beginnings of fuzz on her chin. In her free hand, she held a cardboard sign, its handwritten English as tortured as her husband's rendition of "Stormy Weather": THIS IS MY JOB. i Am New iimigrent from BELORUS. Give me 3 SHEKELS or DOLLAR. Please. Tank You!!!

Gesh dropped five dollars into the battered sax case and the man removed the instrument's reed from his mouth and smiled.

When he arrived back at Marty's apartment, Debbie asked Gesh about his day. Where did he go? Wasn't everything so amazing? Did he see the Western Wall? She had a $20,000 smile that said her father had taken her for braces when Gesh's father had dragged Gesh along to Belmont Park and Aqueduct Racetrack to watch him lose his shirt.

Gesh covered his crooked mouth and answered, "Beer and Minerals."

"What do you mean, 'Beer and Minerals?'" Debbie asked.

"The *shicker* went drinking. I can't believe it," Marty said.

"Didn't you see the Western Wall? You've got to see the Western Wall."

"Why?" Gesh said.

"Why?" Marty said. "Why? Are you a Jew? That's what a Jew does. He visits the Wall, prays and gives it a kiss."

"Leave him alone, Marty."

"It's your heritage, schmuck, your history," Marty added.

"Not my history," Gesh said. "Not my Canyon of Heroes."

"All right," Marty said, patting his cousin on the shoulder in that patronizing way he had. "The Western Wall is where God hangs out. A magic place. Like Coney Island. You got a wish? You write it in a note and stick the note in the wall."

"Then what?" Gesh said.

"Then what?" Marty replied. "You're a Jew. Figure it out."

Gesh placed a paper *kippa* on his head and walked across the polished stone plaza towards the Western Wall. The sun reflected pink and gold from the stones. People milled about and prayed, and the quiet murmur from the black-dressed worshippers rose up into the sky.

He pressed his lips to the cool wall and closed his eyes, wondering if God might answer his wishes. He muttered his wish under his breath, half-embarrassed. I'm not praying; just asking a favor, he thought. Gesh eyed the tiny notes crammed into the cracks between the wall's bright stones. He wanted to read a note or two, but his fingers were clumsy and the notes were gummed together as if by rain or tears. Someone touched Gesh lightly on the shoulder.

"You're looking for something," a man said in an American accent. He was short, with a broad chest like a subway car, ginger-colored beard and waterlogged blue eyes.

"Yeah," Gesh said. "I'm looking for something."

"You are looking for God," the man said, slipping his thumbs under his suspenders. "Where else would you find God? This is his front doorstep. There is a word: *Shechina*. It means, Divine Presence. Don't you feel the *Shechina*? Have you ever laid *tefillin*?"

Gesh hadn't laid much of anything.

"No," Gesh said.

"Better one good deed than a thousand good thoughts," the man said. "You're looking for God."

"I'm looking for a wife," Gesh said, surprising himself.

"Oh." The man paused. He removed his black *kippa* and dabbed with a tissue at the bald patch on his head. "A Jewish wife looks for a good man," he said. "A man who does not wear *tefillin* is simply against God. Now tell me, what sort of woman would want a man who is a sinner?"

Gesh followed the man to a slanted table piled high with books.

"Don't worry, I'm a rabbi. This won't hurt a bit," the man said, smiling behind his beard. "Moshe Yaakov." He extended his hand.

"Gershom. Gesh."

Rabbi Moshe Yaakov placed a small wooden box on Gesh's bicep, and secured the box by winding the leather strap seven times around Gesh's left arm and through his fingers. The rabbi looped another leather strap over Gesh's head so that a wooden box rested on Gesh's fore-head between his eyes.

Gesh felt like an idiot.

"Repeat after me."

When they were done, the rabbi said, "How do you feel?"

"Like crap."

"I understand. Rabbi Jacob said that, 'He who has no wife lives without good, or help, or joy, or blessing, or atonement.' And Rabbi Levi added that 'Such a man has no life.'"

Gesh thought of his father, packing Gesh's things into boxes and marking the cardboard with black ink: GESH'S BOOKS, GESH'S CLOTHES, GESH'S RECORDS. That was his life: easily packed up and put away. He broke down before the rabbi, "I have no life. I'm forty years old. Smell my shirt." Gesh motioned towards his sleeve. "That's my mother's perfume."

"It's all right," the rabbi said, unwinding the leather straps from Gesh's bulging arm. "Before a man marries, his love goes to his parents. When he is married, the love goes to his wife. I'm a matchmaker, Gershom. Laying *tefillin* is the first step to being a good Jew."

"They still have matchmakers?" Gesh said.

"Believe me, Gershom," Rabbi Moshe Yaakov said. "Not only that, we still have *shochatim* and *mohels* and *rebbes*. We even still have God."

Sometime after dark, Gesh wound his way through the narrow streets of the Jewish Quarter in search of the rabbi's home. The moon had risen, and its gleam illuminated the small scrap of paper in his hand; it bore the rabbi's address. Gesh didn't want to be late. He had never been on a date. He had tried once when he was eighteen and had been called a cripple by his dentist's cruel daughter. But now, he felt he had someone in his corner, a go-between, a coach. Rabbi Moshe Yaakov had arranged successful matches hundreds of times before. Gesh found the address painted in blue on a stone wall. He knocked on the steel door.

After a moment, the rabbi answered. He was still wearing his white shirt and suspenders, but now a pair of steel-rimmed glasses were propped on the end of his nose.

"Come in, Gershom," the rabbi said with a smile. "You're just in time."

Gesh ducked his head under the lintel of the doorframe and entered the rabbi's home. The rabbi kissed his fingers and touched them to the *mezuzah* on the doorpost. He gestured for Gesh to do the same.

"What's wrong?"

"I don't know. What if she is not pretty?"

"A man must marry a woman to whom he is attracted."

"What if she is not nice? What if she is too smart for me?"

"For every affliction, silence is the best remedy. Gershom – just look, listen, relax. Come, we'll say a quick prayer."

Rabbi Moshe Yaakov led Gesh into a cluttered living room. "You might want to cover your head, Gershom. It is respectful to always cover your head before God." He handed Gesh a *kippa*.

Afterwards, the rabbi led Gesh down a sloping hallway into a bare room. Two plastic chairs sat in the middle of the unadorned floor. Fluorescent lights buzzed overhead.

"Sit. Rest your leg. She will be here shortly."

After the rabbi left, Gesh noticed a small barred window across the room. It looked out onto street level; he could see people's ankles and calves as they passed. As he sat, plastic chair bending under his weight, he imagined her: a kind, round face, soft lips, brown hair tickling against her shoulders. And her laugh, it would be a laugh like spring that could make flowers bloom and dance. A laugh that could fill the whole world. He would take her smooth hand in his and she would say, "Don't worry, you can hold me tighter, I won't break." They would walk through the dark streets and because he was at her side, she would feel safe for the first time.

Gesh heard laughing behind the window and looked up as two faces disappeared into the darkness. The hideous fluorescent lights buzzed in his ears like drills. A few minutes later, Rabbi Moshe Yaakov knocked on the door and entered.

"My apologies, Gesh," the rabbi said. "The young lady called and won't be able to make it. She has sunstroke."

"Sunstroke?"

"She is terribly sorry," the rabbi said. "You'll come back tomorrow. We can pray again."

"I don't think so," Gesh said, walking up the sloping hallway into the cluttered living room. "I saw her at the window, laughing at me."

"Nonsense. That was just the children. I understand how you feel: lonely, like half a person, like you are not truly whole. Because that is the way a man is when he is not married; half a heart, half a soul, half a brain. He does silly things because he is not yet right in his head. Well, that other half is out there and she is wandering around alone, searching. She's searching for you, Gesh."

"I feel awful."

"How do you think she feels?" Rabbi Moshe Yaakov said.

After reciting a prayer with the rabbi, Gesh returned the next three nights. Each night, he was led to the bare, buzzing room where he sat alone in the bending plastic chair until the rabbi came for him.

"A headache," the rabbi said.

"She must have lost her way," the rabbi consoled the following evening.

"I'm sorry. This one's unclean. She has her cycle."

Baloney, Gesh thought. I'm wasting my time.

"You'll come back for *Shabbos?*" the rabbi said, taking Gesh's arm.

"No," Gesh said.

"A Jew should not be alone for the Sabbath."

"I'm tired of hearing what a Jew should be," Gesh said, removing the *kippa* from his head. "I don't mean any disrespect, Rabbi. But I'm not gonna be coming back."

"Will you say a quick prayer with me?" Rabbi Moshe Yaakov asked. "So we do not part enemies."

"Goodbye," Gesh said, and he walked out into the cool night air.

"All beginnings are difficult," the rabbi called down the lonely street.

Gesh noticed a bank of telephones off the square. In his wallet he found the card bearing his parents' new address. He imagined dialing the number and what he would say to his mother.

"Ma. I got good news. I'm gettin' married, just like you wanted."

"Oh, my God. It's a miracle. Is she Jewish?" his mother would say.

"Yeah, she's Jewish. A Falasha."

"A falafel?" his mother would say. "A what? What did you say, Gesh?"

"A black girl, Ma. From Ethiopia. In Africa."

Gesh was still laughing as he walked through the square, past clustered groups of identically dressed *yeshiva* students eating ice cream cones, and past the barred windows of tourist shops. He left the square and found the quiet side streets where people lived and hung their laundry to dry. He wandered farther still, on dark, downward sloping streets, where skinny cats meowed from the shadows. He could smell vegetables rotting, and then, down a street of shuttered storefronts, he smelled the blood of butchered animals. The streets were vaulted now, and the only view of the moon was through the grated skylights above. Gesh could hear the uneven echo of his feet hitting the stone street. He passed homes loud with television sets, children crying, and laughter. In the open air, minarets rose above him. He passed bored Israeli soldiers slumped in their chairs outside of Jewish homes and said, "*Shalom.*" The stars in the sky seemed impossibly close when Gesh arrived at a street that he recognized from when he'd set out almost two hours earlier.

"Hello," a voice called out. "Hello, friend."

Gesh looked up just as he was upon the little Arab man.

"You are looking for the cathouse. Welcome."

"No," Gesh said. "I'm just walking."

The man was wearing a white straw hat and dark sunglasses. He stepped back a few feet so that he could take a better look at Gesh.

"I make sure you don't get lost," the man said.

"I'm not lost."

"Yes, yes. You are looking for the cathouse. This way. This way. You come with me. Welcome."

"I'm not lost. I am meeting a friend."

"Yes, you are. This is the Way of Sorrows. In the day, they look for Christ. In the night, they look for love. The night is a happy time on the Way of Sorrows. No one is disappointed. I will show you your friend."

"I have to go," Gesh said.

"You're not virgin, are you? Are you homo? There's young boys near the Tower of the Stork."

"I'm not gay."

"But you are lonely. Maybe very lonely," the Arab man said. "I can help you."

Gesh finally agreed to follow the little man and they turned off Via Dolorosa and up a rough stone street that was as dark as a cave. The little man pushed open a door and then he and Gesh were inside the darkened room, lit only by the spastic flash of a black and white television. Two young women, wearing matching pink hot pants and blond wigs, sat on a plastic-covered couch playing backgammon. They looked up and then back down. An older, heavy woman, wearing leopard-print tights and a matching headscarf, stared at the television and did not seem to notice that Gesh and the Arab man had entered. The room smelled of cheap incense and sweat.

"Bang, bang," the little man said, taking off his straw hat. "Go on."

This ain't sexy, Gesh thought.

"Go on, lucky man," the little Arab said.

"But they're busy."

"No, no. They're waiting for you. Go. *Yala!*" And he slapped Gesh on the rump.

Gesh slowly walked over to the young girls in hot pants.

"Hi," Gesh said. "Who's winning?"

Nothing. Just the rattle of dice.

The little man said something in Arabic that Gesh did not understand.

"Sit with them," the man said.

Gesh sank into the couch between the older woman and one of the backgammon players.

"Now what?" Gesh asked. He could feel his forehead growing with embarrassment.

"The money. You must give the money."

Gesh handed some wrinkled bills to each of the girls. The blondes quickly snatched up their share and put the money under their wigs. The older woman crumpled the bills in a ball and continued to watch the TV.

Gesh heard the theme music from *Dallas* and the peeling sound of the girls' behinds unsticking from the plastic couch. They were up and they were gone, without even a moan. The older woman also stood up and walked out of the room.

"What happened?" Gesh said.

"Show's over, friend. Tomorrow you bang again?"

The following day, Gesh returned to Zion Square and the BEER & MINERALS stand. For a while, he watched the strange faces passing before him. Then Rabbi Moshe Yaakov appeared out of the crowd, his side-curls swinging in the air as he walked. Here he comes again to peddle his horseshit religion, Gesh thought.

"*Baruch HaShem*. I'm glad I found you, Gershom."

Gesh took a sip of his juice but did not look up at the rabbi.

"What's the matter? You don't look well," the rabbi said.

"Haven't you noticed?" Gesh said. "I never look well."

"Look at me. How do you think I looked before I wore these clothes?" the rabbi asked, pulling on his *tzitzis* and tugging on his *kippa*.

"You don't understand," Gesh said, sneezing, with great force, into his hand.

The rabbi said a quick prayer under his breath, his watery blue eyes growing large.

"What was that?" Gesh asked.

"A prayer. For the sneeze."

"You pray for that?"

"Gershom, that is just one of the wonders of Judaism. There are prayers for the first flowers in spring, there are prayers you say when lightning strikes, and when thunder booms across the sky. There are prayers for love and there are prayers for prayers. There is even a prayer for passing gas."

"Really?" Gesh said, smiling. "For farting?"

"An unholy wind," the rabbi said, laughing.

"Why me?" Gesh said after a moment, pulling on the edge of his nose. "I'm just a *schlepper*."

"God loves *schleppers*, too."

"Then God must be blind."

The rabbi pulled a knitted *kippa* from his coat pocket and handed it to Gesh. It lay in Gesh's palm like one of those fancy doilies his mother used when she served cocktails to company.

"Try it on," the rabbi said. "Look, it has your name on it."

The name GERSHOM was embroidered into the stitching of the *kippa*.

"I can't wear this," Gesh said.

"Why not?"

Gesh shrugged, and his shoulders felt heavy.

"That's not a good enough reason." The rabbi turned and stretched out his arm towards the people walking in the square. "Look at those people wandering through life without direction. Without anyone to guide them. Do you want to live like that?"

Gesh looked at the passing parade and saw laughter, hope and beauty. "Yes," Gesh said. "Yes."

"Come and see me again this evening. I promise you, I have found your *beshert*. Your missing half. I promise she will be there, Gershom."

Gesh went, but he didn't wear the gift the rabbi had given him.

"She is waiting for you. Join me first for a prayer."

Gesh emerged from the fluorescent-lit room a few moments later. The rabbi, who was waiting at the end of the hall, raised his eyebrows. "She is very beautiful, Gershom. What do you think?"

"She doesn't speak English," Gesh said. "And she's five months pregnant if she's a day."

"You didn't like the way she looked? She's very smart," the rabbi said. "She studied nursing in Moscow."

Zhanna Joseferovna was attractive enough that Gesh had imagined making love to her through a hole in a sheet the way he had heard religious Jews do it. And he imagined Rabbi Moshe Yaakov watching them through a hole in the wall, and up in the sky, he imagined God parting the clouds, watching over all his children.

"It doesn't feel right. I didn't understand a word she said."

"Love is about understanding what you don't understand, Gershom. When Ruth the Moabite came to Boaz, she came from a distant land, and eventually begat King David."

"Goodbye," Gesh said, walking away.

"A nice Jewish baby needs a nice Jewish father. Love will grow like a seed," the rabbi called after him. "If you give it time."

A load of bull, Gesh thought.

He felt closed in, claustrophobic within the walls of the Old City, so he wandered up through the Arab *souk* and out through Jaffa Gate into the new city. He walked farther and farther away from the rabbi and his empty buzzing room, into neighborhoods Gesh had never before seen. He wandered into a lush garden community and watched the moon follow him through the tree branches. The air was cool and smelled of flowers. As he turned the corner onto a smaller street where cars were parked along the sidewalks, he heard an old woman calling out in Hebrew. It sounded like she was shouting for her cat. Gesh had seen a few skinny cats picking through garbage cans. He called to the woman in English that maybe he had seen her cat.

"Teddy, is that you? Is that you walking in the street?"

Gesh was close enough now that he could see she was sitting at the window with her bare arms propped on the ledge.

"Hello," Gesh called.

"Teddy, is it really you at last?"

"Lady, I don't know—"

"Don't shout at me from the street, Teddy. Come inside and speak to me."

"*Sheket!*" someone cried from across the street.

"No!" the woman screamed. "You be quiet. Teddy is home."

"No, you be quiet," the voice from across the street called. "Crazy lady."

Gesh opened a small iron gate and walked up the dark stone path, nearly tripping on the uneven stones.

"Lady, I—"

"Teddy, where have you been? I've been worried for you."

Gesh stood under the window now, and in the moonlight he could see from her milky cataracts that she was blind.

She leaned forward, her palms pressing on the ledge. "Teddy, it is you?" she whispered. "Come in, the door is not locked. Up the stairs and to the left."

"Quiet, lady," the voice called from across the street. "You are waking the dead."

Gesh mounted the stairs.

The old woman stood in the doorway, slowly rocking back and forth, mumbling, "Teddy, Teddy, Teddy. " She was slim, her face worn and wrinkled from the years. Her white hair was tied back behind her head. "Teddy." She reached out to Gesh, and with more force than he expected, she pulled him to her and wrapped her thin arms around him. "You have grown," she said, a tear running down her cracked cheek.

She poured him a glass of juice and sat near him on the couch. Though she was blind, she moved around the apartment with a comfort that suggested she had known every inch of it for a very long time. For a few moments, they sat in silence in the darkened living room, drinking their juice. Gesh noticed jars of pills and several half-empty glasses of water spread out on the low coffee table. A small radio played quietly from the darkness of a cluttered bookshelf.

"Lady, listen—"

"Mama," she said. "You call me Mama, remember?" She spoke English in a thick European accent that

Gesh could not place. "I was afraid you got married and went away. You didn't forget about me, Teddy."

Gesh felt something in his stomach; it was like a fist clenching and unclenching. "I didn't forget about you," he said at last. And a bright smile broke across her face.

As his eyes adjusted to the dim light, he saw that in each of the photographs on the wall was a young air force pilot, in uniform, stern, beside his plane, or smiling broadly with friends. He was handsome and confident, full of swagger and the belief that the world was his. The photos were old, washed out by time, and Gesh knew that this young man had died long ago in one of Israel's many wars. Although the woman could not see the photographs, Gesh could tell by how crookedly they hung on the wall that they were frequently loved and caressed by her worn fingers.

The old woman moved close to him on the couch and stroked his cheek with her right hand. "Teddy," she said. "Tell me, where have you been?"

Gesh heard his heart beating loudly in his chest. "I've been flying."

"Yes, yes," the woman said. "Tell me to where."

Her face was so close to his that her sour breath stung his nostrils.

"Africa," he said, after a moment.

He heard her sigh deeply. "Yes," she said. "Africa."

Gesh swallowed deeply, his Adam's apple thick in his throat. "I saw lions and tigers, elephants. And big colorful birds in the jungle."

"Tell me about the birds," she said.

"They were red and blue and purple – every color you can imagine," Gesh said. "And they sang the most beautiful songs."

"Sing one," she said.

"Mama," Gesh said. "They are too beautiful for me to sing to you."

"Teddy, please."

Gesh hummed the tune to an old Broadway number that his mother had loved when he was a child.

"Your voice is still like an angel's, Teddy. Do you remember singing 'Hatikvah' on Independence Day, how all the girls came and listened to my Teddy, and said that one day they would marry you?"

"Yes," Gesh lied.

"Sing 'Hatikvah' for me now."

"Mama," Gesh said. "It's late."

"I have missed you so much. Please sing 'Hatikvah' for me."

"All right," Gesh said, after a moment. He didn't know the words or the tune. Softly, he sang, "Take Me Out to the Ballgame," the only song in the world to which he knew all the lyrics.

When he was finished singing, Gesh noticed that the old woman had fallen asleep in his lap, a placid smile playing across her wrinkled face. In the silence of the living room, Gesh could hear the lonely sound of a cat mewling outside, and the wind brushing through the trees, and he felt for the first time in a long time that he was worth something. He pulled a thin blanket from the back of the couch and draped it over the old woman's sleeping form. She stirred, opened her eyes, and seemed, to Gesh, to see something in him beyond the power of sight.

She grabbed his wrist with incredible force and whispered, "My sweet baby. Don't ever leave me again."

Gesh leaned over and kissed her softly on the cheek. "I won't, Mama, I won't."

The Last Five-Year Plan

Irving Blumenfield woke from a dreamless sleep with one shining word on his pale lips: diamonds. His alarm clock flashed vague ruby-red digits in the cool crystalline darkness that marked the no man's land between late evening and very early morning. He stretched himself across the empty bed, thinking. Diamonds. Why diamonds? His wife had died of a sudden stroke three years earlier, and there was no new woman in his life to buy for. He had made millions, nearly a billion in fact, transforming high-rises into parking lots and parking lots back into high-rises. His success had, in part, come from heeding similar nocturnal calls. But diamonds? Blumenfield had never dealt with precious gems; he thought that the South Africans were insufferable pricks and that the Hasidim on 47th Street were nothing but a bunch of money-laundering crooks who would be only too happy to pick the pocket of the President and CEO of Blumenfield Corp., National Chairman of Project Israel and founder of the nascent Jewish Baseball Hall of Fame. Yes, Blumenfield laughed, it would be a feather in their fedoras if they could get me. But you've got to wake up pretty early to screw Irving Blumenfield.

It was a crisp autumn day in early October, the High Holidays over and the World Series yet to come. The sun was setting, and Blumenfield was reclining in his midtown office tower, his high definition television tuned to four split-screened stations, when he suddenly understood that it was not the God of Finance who had whispered in his ear the night before, no, this time he knew it had been the God upstairs, the God of Judgment, who, just last week, had inscribed Blumenfield into the Book of Life for another year.

"Dot," he called into his intercom. "Send Josh in here."

His assistant was a tall, lean Columbia graduate who had wowed Blumenfield with his knowledge of baseball, history and politics two years earlier at a wedding on Long Island. Blumenfield had given Josh a Confederate two-dollar bill emblazoned with the face of Judah P. Benjamin, the Jewish Secretary of State under Jefferson Davis, as a gift for being a man of quality, despite Josh's Columbia education. In between dinner and dessert, Blumenfield offered him the job; Josh began the following Monday. It was not uncommon for the two of them to work late into the evening, when the empty windows of the adjacent office towers burned a dull, numb yellow, a cleaning woman periodically appearing at a window, dragging her burden over the carpets and floors of the office cubicles.

"Josh," Blumenfield said, his gruff voice bending even the softest syllable into a reproachful growl. "Sit down. I want to talk to you."

"Mr. Blumenfield, if it's about the contracts—"

"Fuck the contracts. Sit."

"Yes, Mr. Blumenfield."

Blumenfield sat beneath a framed baseball jersey – white, starched, autographed, it once belonged to the great Hank Greenberg. It seemed to float above Blumenfield, arms outstretched like a guardian angel.

Blumenfield tilted back in his swivel chair, his out-sized glasses pressed against his face, giving the illusion that his quickly darting eyes were Siamese fighting fish zipping back and forth in their solitary bowls.

"Josh, do you think I'm a good person? Am I a good man, someone who will leave this world a better place than when he came in?"

"Of course."

"Don't bullshit me. No bullshit. All right. It's enough I have three no-good lying kids. I need another phony like I need roller-skates."

Josh cleared his throat and straightened his tie. "Some would say that it's wrong to block a river view from 478 tenants with a seventy-story structure. But I believe that the greater good is served by the building you've built. Now, more people have a view of the river, and on a clear day they can see the Atlantic. And evictions? All in the name of progress. People always find somewhere to live."

"And I got stinking, filthy rich," Blumenfield interrupted.

"And we keep reaching higher," Josh corrected. "That's human nature. Would you suggest for one minute that we leave two empty holes in Lower Manhattan because of the feelings of a few activist widows? We move forward, we progress. You're not a bad man," Josh said. "I understand you, Mr. Blumenfield."

"I know you do."

"You're a visionary."

"Visionary," Blumenfield whispered in his grainy voice. "You know when Stalin was alive, millions of people thought Papa Joe was a good man and a visionary." He paused. "How many five-year plans can I have left to make things right?" Blumenfield cleared the emotion from his throat. "I'm doomed, I know it." Blumenfield leaned forward. "My kids won't speak to me. I've never seen my grandchildren. Marilyn is dead. I know mayors, heads of state, corporate leaders, the rich, the famous. I am respected – and feared. Do you know, Josh, that I consider you my closest friend in the entire world?"

"Thank you, Mr. Blumenfield."

Blumenfield slumped in his chair. "I paid you a goddamn compliment. Call me Irving at least."

"Irving?"

"Josh," Blumenfield said dolorously.

"What's the matter? You don't seem right today."

"One morning you wake up and you see a face in the mirror you don't recognize, and it reminds you that you're old and broken and you're beyond all renovation, and the wrecking ball is coming." He picked up the remote for the television and flipped stations. The screen divided from four to eight to twelve, flashing a dozen incongruous images. An old sitcom appeared on one screen, an advertisement for feminine hygiene on another. In the top right frame, on a 24-hour news station, several dozen teenagers pelted rocks at an approaching Israeli Jeep, and then ducked for cover as rubber-tipped bullets screamed in their direction.

Blumenfield picked up an autographed baseball from his desk and absentmindedly tossed it from hand to hand. "Some of those kids can throw," he said. "Look at the arm on that kid, the mechanics. I'll bet he can throw one of these through a brick wall."

"Or your head," Josh said.

"That's despair," Blumenfield said. "You've seen what despair did to property values in the South Bronx."

"As long as Yankee Stadium is there, there's still hope," Josh replied.

Another news story appeared on the screen.

Blumenfield stood up and, without warning, tossed the baseball at Josh. "Nice catch." He stepped around his desk and put his hands on Josh's shoulders. "Nice catch," he repeated, but softly this time. He began to rub out the knots in Josh's shoulders, Blumenfield's firm hands kneading the muscles with his newly manicured fingers. "Josh," he began, dropping his hands. "I want to ask you something, and I want to say up front that you can say no, and that I won't be angry or upset. This is entirely up to you."

"What is it?" Josh's Adam's apple bobbed up and down as he swallowed air.

"I want you to say *Kaddish* for me when I'm gone. Not just once, but the whole works. I want you to remember me and honor me, so I'm not forgotten."

"Of course," Josh said. "But you're not going to die."

"We're all going to die," Blumenfield said. "It's just a matter of timing and location."

Josh quickly snapped the ball back to Blumenfield, who reached out his hand and plucked the ball from the air.

Josh smiled. "You've still got a lot left in you."

"You hungry, kid?"

"I could eat something."

"Good. Call Happy Garden and have them send up the usual."

They sat on the floor before the giant television screen, eating pineapple chicken and chop suey out of paper cartons. Josh had found a dusty magnum of champagne beneath Dot's desk – Blumenfield had given it to her last year to mark thirty years of service to the real estate mogul. Josh popped the cork, spraying Blumenfield with foam.

"Careful," Blumenfield growled. "This is the suit I'm going to be buried in."

"Have a drink."

"All right. A toast," Blumenfield said.

"To the future." Josh raised his glass.

"To the future."

They drank.

And they drank.

"Can you believe this goddamn fortune," Blumen-field slurred. "Learn Chinese. What do I want with Chinese? Aren't fortunes supposed to tell you something about your future? You're going to be a star, Josh. Your fortune backs me up all the way. But me, I'm destined for remedial Chinese so I can learn to say chop suey in its original language."

Josh laughed and turned over the scrap of paper. "Your fortune's on the other side. It says, 'You're a diamond in the rough.'"

"Well, thank you very much, Confucius."

The television flashed before them, and the news story of the stone-throwing Palestinians reappeared in the top right-hand corner. That was when Blumenfield, as if struck in the temple by one of those stones, realized what he needed to do. Diamonds, yes. Baseball diamonds. That was what the nocturnal voice had been try-ing to tell him. His legacy lay in the cultivation of base-ball diamonds. Both the Polo Grounds and Ebbets Field had become housing project slums; why couldn't a war zone become a baseball diamond?

"Josh, I've got an idea. Look at those kids throwing stones. Look at that anger. I've got the solution. I found the answer. Write this down quick. Just write."

Josh grabbed a notebook off of Blumenfield's desk.

"Okay. The power of baseball. Just follow me. Confederate and Union soldiers, gentlemen, farm boys, they all played baseball in the pastures and fields – the same fields that, not long before, had been killing fields.

That was one thing that the Union men and the rebels could agree on: they all loved baseball. They could battle on the field without killing anyone. Baseball was the great democratizer, a place where men earned their place on the team not because of rank, or social class, but because of skill." Blumenfield gestured to the starched, white shirt hovering above them. "Look at Hammerin' Hank. Look at Jackie Robinson: he was the son of sharecroppers, and now he's got his own postage stamp and a plaque in Cooperstown. Baseball did more to desegregate America in the middle of the twentieth century than any war. Not only that, it's been a way for urban blacks to escape the ghetto."

"What are you talking about?"

"And, the Japanese. After WWII, they had plenty of reasons to hate the Americans who had nuked their cities, deposed their emperor and occupied their country. So why is it that Japan and America have been at peace ever since?"

"I don't follow," Josh said.

"Who holds the all-time home run world record? Forget Aaron or Ruth."

"Sadaharu Oh," Josh responded. "868."

"Exactly. The Japanese channeled their energies into baseball instead of war and conquest, and now there are Matsuis and Nomos and Suzukis on almost every major league team. No country that plays baseball has ever gone to war against another country that plays baseball," Blumenfield concluded.

"Are you forgetting Grenada? Or the US-backed Contras in Nicaragua? How about that Fidel Castro was a left-handed pitcher who tried out for the Washington Senators? Do you remember the Cuban missile crisis?"

"You're not listening, smarty-pants. If people are playing baseball, they're not out killing Israelis."

"What are you talking about?"

"My peace plan. Baseball for the Palestinians. Fuck bread and circuses. I say baseball."

"You're joking," Josh said.

"If you will it, it is no dream. What do you think people said when Herzl vowed he'd make the desert bloom? Who would have thought Eliezer Ben-Yehuda could ever have revived a dead desert language that today, over five million people speak? Here's my five-year plan: a lasting Israeli-Palestinian peace accord, a Palestinian baseball team in the next Summer Olympics, my final legacy cemented in history."

"You're drunk," Josh said.

"I've never felt better."

"Do you think it's a coincidence that the Hebrew word for *bullet* and *ball* are the same, Mr. Blumenfield?"

"It's Irving, you Ivy League putz. You think I made a billion dollars from nothing with idiot ideas?"

"No."

"Then are you with me?"

"What about the security fence keeping the Palestinians out of Israel?"

"One morning the people awoke to find that their bogeyman had become a Green Monster."

Josh smiled. "Buying the land for the baseball diamonds shouldn't be too difficult."

"Yes, yes," Blumenfield said. "We will have an exhibition game on Opening Day with Jewish major leaguers playing the new Palestinian squad. We can get Koufax to throw out the first pitch. Carew can coach."

"You can't do it on Opening Day. The major leaguers will be here, playing for their teams on Opening Day. And who is going to teach the Palestinians how to play? Baseball is not an easy game."

Blumenfield scoffed. "Hit, run, throw. People have been clubbing spheres since Cain killed Abel. It's track and field with props and a plot. Tell me, who doesn't understand the desire to go home?"

"I don't like the way this sounds," Josh said. "Refugees, the right of return—"

"We'll work it out," Blumenfield said. "Now, get on the horn and make this happen."

One hundred *dunums* of land was easy enough for a man like Irving Blumenfield to acquire. He paid good money for the gnarled olive groves and tattered goat pastures; good enough, considering his threat: that Israeli bulldozers would level the land for security purposes, with no hope on earth of remuneration. One hundred *dunums*, twenty-five acres of land – outside Bethlehem, Ramallah, Abu Dis and Hebron – would mark the footprints of the first baseball diamonds for the Millennium

Peace League. Stadiums were also to be built in six Israeli cities on public land; this, Blumenfield had negotiated separately.

"According to plan," Blumenfield counseled the day that the papers were signed and the deeds transferred to him.

"If you build it, they will come," Josh said, barely concealing his sarcasm.

"Fifty-percent unemployment, despair everywhere. They'll goddamn well come. I'll subsidize everything from peanuts to Crackerjacks. And remember, this is a game, and people love to play games. Imagine baseball cards instead of suicide martyr posters."

"But this isn't America. There are certain sensitivities you have to consider."

"When have I ever done that?" Blumenfield asked. "Sensitivities are for the weak and Irving Blumenfield has not built a billion-dollar empire on weakness. And look how the new retro stadiums have brought down-towns back to life – Cleveland, Baltimore, Pittsburgh. We can do the same for the Palestinians."

"This is quixotic at best," Josh interrupted. "Try-ing to reconfigure the paradigm in this manner is like hitting a square peg into a round hole. It will never work."

"Josh, don't take the shine off this. I haven't felt this alive since—" He paused and blinked back a tear. "It will work," Blumenfield continued. "If you pound hard enough and never let up, it will work."

And so, Blumenfield was secretly surprised by the reactions of both Israelis and Palestinians. Protests sprung up across the country, some violent, some not. Dr. Ashrawi made the rounds on the 24-hour news networks, calling Blumenfield's plan nothing but an Israeli land grab: "You need look no further than his own Project Israel, which has housed tens of thousands of new Russian immigrants on Palestinian land. The only difference now is that he has crossed the 1967 line." A prominent Muslim cleric decried the excavation for the stadium near Hebron that unearthed the pious bones of a sixteenth century saint who was believed to be a direct descendent of the Prophet Mohammed himself. The Israeli left called Blumenfield a fanatic, the greatest threat to peace and stability in the Middle East; meanwhile, the settler movement on the West Bank claimed the land their own, as God promised Abraham all those years ago. They rolled their caravans to the very edge of Blumenfield's property and, in a cold rain, raised the Israeli Star of David, with a loud and proud *Shehechiyanu*.

Blumenfield thought of his friend Robert Moses, New York's master builder. Had twenty-five years passed that quickly? It seemed that everybody Blumenfield knew was dead or dying now. You blink your eyes and you're a mile closer to the grave, and all the steel and glass that you have raised to the heavens does nothing, nothing at all to postpone that day. Blumenfield had admired and privately envied Moses, who had torn down useless slums, eyesores in Manhattan, to build Stuyvesant Town,

Lincoln Center, the United Nations, the FDR highway –
bridges, and more highways, hundreds of miles of highways, finally bringing New York City and its five boroughs into the twentieth century. He had often wished
that he could make a difference the way Robert Moses
had; Blumenfield's high-rises were glittering monuments
to nothing that signified nothing. But now, Blumenfield
himself was healing the rifts in the fabric of the world.
He thought back to how Moses had been vilified for
ignoring historic preservation and destroying neighborhood life, how he had been scandalized for transferring
blacks and Puerto Ricans from their homes to his new
housing projects in Brooklyn and the Bronx, how he had
been blasted for eviscerating the boroughs with his con-
crete highways. Even Blumenfield had cursed him half a
century ago for nixing the stadium plan that would have
kept the hated Dodgers in Brooklyn, and then for demol-
ishing the Polo Grounds after the Giants moved west.
But Moses had endured, and now, nobody was clamoring for the old days when New York had been an open
cesspool, an island on a filthy stream drifting off the
coast of America. Now, cries of 'Play Ball!' rang out
from major-league baseball stadiums stretching from the
Atlantic all the way to the Pacific.

The land of the West Bank was nothing but an eye-
sore, anyway: hilly, rocky, windswept, sun-baked, and far
from any viable source of water. No oil or precious minerals lay beneath its earth and few crops sprung from its
haunted soil. Blumenfield felt that people who sentimen-

tally clung to those pimply hilltops had been sold a line that only a master salesman could push once in a thousand years. Blumenfield was bent on bringing baseball to that scarred land to erase hundreds of years of pain and misery. Hadn't Moses brought highways to a walking city, housing to the poor, bridges to an urban archipelago, order to chaos? Hadn't he converted twelve hundred acres of swamp in Flushing, Queens, into a grand fairground and then turned that fairground into the home of the New York Mets? He had been defamed, pilloried and slandered, but he pressed on and his legacy was felt every day by nearly eight million New Yorkers.

The week after Thanksgiving, Blumenfield's lawyer phoned. "Green and Lieberthal are out."

"What about the bodybuilder, Kaplan?"

"It's Kapler, and he's out as well."

"What in the goddamn hell is going on, Sy? It's an exhibition game. Don't these overpaid babies believe in peace and coexistence?"

"They do, Irving. That's the problem. This whole cockeyed plan of yours is turning into a real mess. To a man, they think March 30th is a mistake. That's Land Day for the Palestinians; it commemorates Israeli land confiscations since the founding of the state."

"Ancient history," Blumenfield said.

"Is it, Irving? We're talking about a land where time is marked in centuries, not years. The only reason the government is allowing these stadiums to be built is because you've been such a good friend to the State of

Israel. But honestly, this goes against their better judgment."

"I'll tell you about judgment."

"The Palestinians don't want baseball on their pastures and olive groves any more than they want Walmart or Disneyland."

"But the game is for them," Blumenfield said.

"That's like building a statue of Hitler in the middle of Tel Aviv and saying, 'It's made of gold.'"

"Cut the hyperbole, Sy. It's a fucking game. I'm trying to make a change, give the day new meaning, bring sunlight to the darkness and all that bullshit."

"What's your angle, Irv? What do you really want? I've known you too long to believe this is just about baseball."

"I want to bring peace."

"And what can that possibly mean to you?"

"The end of hostilities," Blumenfield said flatly, leaving no room for interpretation.

There was silence on the other end of the line, and then Blumenfield's lawyer said, "I'll level with you, Irving. Men far, far greater and wiser than you have tried and failed. What makes you so special?"

It stung Blumenfield to hear those words. He was not used to people doubting him. There had, in fact, been a time when he would have immediately dismissed his lawyer for such impudent comments. But he was tired and he remembered what his late friend Robert Moses said during times of adversity. He repeated those words almost verbatim to his lawyer. "This is where the skeptic finds chaos and the believer further evidence that the hand that made us is Divine."

"I hope you're joking, Irv, because the robes don't fit. This messianic business just ain't your bag."

A few days after the ball dropped in Times Square – during that bleak hangover period when dirty snow fills the gutters and the flashing colored lights strung throughout the city are seedy, mocking baubles signifying another festive season unfulfilled – Blumenfield went to see his doctor. He had been exhaustively traveling around the country in search of semi-pro and college players who could prove that they were at least one-half Jewish: a starting nine for his Opening Day. He was willing to pay whatever it took, but he found few takers, given that three Palestinian laborers, who had been laying the foundation for the Abu Dis field, were found lynched with Arabic notes around their broken necks, calling them collaborators. Additionally, the Hebron baseball diamond had become a tent city for one hundred Jewish families claiming that the land was natural expansion, and a future suburb of Kiryat Arba. Both stories had made international headlines. The Israeli army tried to remove the squatters, but refused to fire live ammunition on their own people. By mid-January, only three players, benchwarmers from obscure junior colleges, had signed on.

The chest pains began in Oaxaca. Josh had unearthed a slugging first baseman in the Mexican League, nicknamed El Rabino, The Rabbi, who claimed to be descended from Spanish Marranos. Blumenfield was invited to eat plantain and rattlesnake, while Josh translated for El Rabino. Blumenfield had never seen a Jew who shared a likeness with El Rabino; he had a fierce gold tooth in the front of his mouth, and a bone-white luminescent scar across his neck that provided the illusion that his square block of a head had been removed with some violence and then replaced, slightly off center.

"One million dollars," Josh communicated.

Blumenfield mopped his brow and said, "Tell him to go fuck himself."

Josh said something in Spanish and El Rabino responded, his heavy-pored, burnished face breaking into a smile. Blumenfield made out the familiar-sounding words, *béisbol* and *Judaísmo*.

"He says for a fellow Jew he'll do it for $600,000."

Blumenfield rose to leave, but El Rabino clamped a heavy hand to Josh's thin waist as if he were about to pick Josh up and swing him like a Louisville Slugger. He barked out something in Spanish that sounded like he was done negotiating.

"$400,000," Josh said, squirming from El Rabino's iron grip.

How had it come to this? Blumenfield had had visions of the greatest Jewish players on earth tutoring their Palestinian cousins in the fine art of bunting, running and catching, modeling a graceful home-run trot, a 12-6 curveball. Instead, here he was, in a distant Mexican province, about to offer a quarter of a million dollars to this bandit called El Rabino, who had no more *neshama* than the rattlesnake that lay curled like a whip on Blumenfield's chipped plate. "$250,000," Blumenfield countered at last.

"Okay," El Rabino said. "Okay. *Bueno.*"

"He wants you to eat," Josh said after a moment of silence in which Blumenfield felt that never, in his seventy-eight years on earth, had he been hustled so badly. And he, like a fool, had just let it happen. But he felt that his time on earth was running out; he couldn't afford to play hardball with El Rabino and risk blowing his last chance to make good.

"I'm not eating this," Blumenfield said, pushing the plate away. "It's staring at me."

"He says you must."

By the look in El Rabino's black eyes, Blumenfield felt that the Mexican meant it.

"Tell him I only eat kosher," Blumenfield said.

A moment later, Josh relayed that the snake was kosher.

"One bite," Blumenfield said, "and then we're leaving this pisshole forever."

That night, he felt a giant foot stepping on his chest, squeezing the air out of his lungs. His feet and hands were pins and needles, his left arm, a useless piece of lumber. He called out for Josh but no voice came. He called out again and still no voice came. Then, Blumenfield did something he had never done before: he called out for God. But no voice came. When he woke in the morning, his chest felt like a wrung-out towel, his lungs like ash. He had wet the bed. The patterned wallpaper depicting jaunty skeletons celebrating the Day of the Dead mocked him. "*Usted esta muerto*," the skeletons whispered. "*Usted esta muerto.*"

When Josh knocked on Blumenfield's door, Irving buried his head under his pillow, too ashamed to answer.

"Montezuma's Revenge," Josh said later, after the maid had unlocked the door. "I was up half the night painting the porcelain."

"It's not Montezuma," Blumenfield said. "It's the Angel of Death. I can feel his eyes all over me right now. Ice water and fire."

Josh reached out a hand to comfort him, but Blumenfield screamed, wide-eyed, "Don't touch me."

"We've got to get you home to see your doctor."

Dr. Brownstein told Blumenfield that his heart rate was up, his blood pressure off the charts, that if he didn't pace himself, the stress would kill him.

Before long, Blumenfield had recovered somewhat and was back to his prickly self. "Stress," he said. "That's nothing but New Age psychobabble. Does that explain the chills, the hot chills like a knife under my ribs? I've never felt anything like it before."

"It could have been food poisoning," Josh offered.

"Could have been?" Blumenfield said. "Isn't there anything that you know for certain?"

"I know for certain that you have to slow down."

Blumenfield had not made a billion dollars by slowing down to attend to the whims of his body. And so, he spent the next month traveling with a searing coal in his chest as he interviewed Jewish ballplayers from Maine to California. He felt that the lifelong internal dialogue between him and his chugging heart was changing, transforming in a way that frightened him. In the past, his heart had thumped back in response to any exertion, no matter how strenuous. Now, it dripped like a leaking faucet. He realized that his heart was not a clock in sync with the rhythms of his body, but a timer winding down to meet an appointment that he had had scheduled for a long time.

One night, in a motel room in La Jolla, Blumenfield saw his own picture appear on the television screen; the newscaster went on to report the body count from the latest rioting in the West Bank. Four more people had died protesting the perceived confiscation of land. "Don't these people understand anything?" Blumenfield muttered to himself. "The Japanese understood. Why can't you understand that baseball is my gift to you?"

He felt his heart clench mid-thought; the pain in his chest was so furious that he actually called out for his mother, an instinct he hadn't felt since he was a small child. In fact, he had forgotten that he used to call her Mumma, that in those days, she would appear in an instant to stroke his forehead and ease whatever it was that had pained him. But now, as the long-forgotten words escaped his lips, he knew that he was completely alone in this world, and that the eyes of the world to come were already all over him like the hungry lips of a new lover. He phoned Josh but got voice mail. How can Josh sound so happy and bright, while my life is ticking away?

Blumenfield closed his eyes and thought of all the things that had brought him the most joy in life: his first kiss with Marilyn at the Jersey Shore, sloppy and cotton-candy sweet; Bobby Thomson's "Shot Heard 'Round the World"; Israel's stunning victory in the Six-Day War; the day Mayor Lindsay had given him the key to the city; the completion of Blumenfield Towers; the sale of Blumen-field Towers at a four hundred percent profit; the first burst of morning exploding over the Red Sea as Blumen-field closed a deal in Sharm el Sheik, the exhilarating whisper of the salt air on his face. The world had been his; he could do no wrong. He thought of the time he watched a honeybee pollinating a red rose. He thought of the time he saw his older sister, twenty years in the ground now, through her bedroom window – how he'd watched in wonderment as she slipped a training bra over her boyish chest. He thought of Saturday matinees, the first home run of the year and the last, the secret thrill of decipher-ing Giants' box scores – a discovery that made him feel as though he'd accessed a mysterious new language that revealed everything. He thought of the smell after sum-mer rain in the city, and the forbidden taste of his moth-er's baking chocolate. He thought of the time he stopped a man from jumping from the Manhattan Bridge; it had made Blumenfield feel reborn twice over, as though he were the proprietor of not one but two souls. As he lay in the darkness, he realized that he had not included the births of his three children in the replay of his most joyous moments. But he had loved them all desperately, once. Then, as the valves of his heart began to relax, allowing blood to pass again into the main chamber, Blumenfield remembered: he had not been present for the births of his three children. Business had always called at the last minute. No amount of cash that he showered on his children had ever been enough to make them understand that the work he was doing was for them.

But, Blumenfield had to ask himself, if he had sacrificed his relationship with his children to better provide for them, why was it that he had cut them from his will like a tumor after Marilyn had died? Why was it that now, in his waning years, he was so stubbornly clinging to his pride when he could cling to his flesh and blood?

I'm a foolish old man, he thought. These thoughts occurred to him more and more frequently, but only very late at night or very early in the morning.

He picked up the telephone. His oldest daughter lived up the coast in Los Angeles and he asked the operator to connect him. Rhonda's useless Gentile husband answered. "Where is she?" Blumenfield growled.

"Who is it?"

The schmuck had refused to come to Marilyn's funeral, and now this insult. Who the fuck do you think it is, Blumenfield silently raged. The man in the moon?

"It's me," he said, softening. "Her father." He did not want to start another fight.

"I think I'm dying," he said, when Rhonda finally picked up the phone.

"How can you call after all this time and say that?"

"I'm sorry," he said.

"Too late for sorry."

"Pussycat," he said.

"Don't call me that," she said.

"I want to come see you."

"You're already dead to me. Self-preservation, all right? You know how many times I let my guard down to love you, and you just walked away?"

"Just let's give it one more try. Me as your dad, you as my daughter." Like old times. He wanted to say the words but thought better of it.

"I saw you on the news, and I want to let you know that I think what you're doing to those poor people is disgusting and reprehensible." She hung up the phone.

Like the child she would always be, she would never understand.

Blumenfield knew that there was no point in trying to contact his other two children; the three of them were worse *yentas* than a sewing circle and seemed to think from one central brain. He realized that he'd better get back to work or be stranded alone on the cold shoulder of eternity.

Blumenfield's inexhaustible will drove him through the rest of the winter, up and down the coast, from east to west; he strode around like a gamecock, making deals, setting his roster. His will had never let him down before. If he willed something to happen, it happened; the forces of creation converging at the diamond-sharp nexus of his energy and desire.

But those bullying close-the-deal monologues he found himself engaged in once again resembled, often to the very word, disputes he had conducted over the past seventy years, as if he were re-dramatizing his entire life in living color, and in his browbeaten interlocutors, he saw the faces of those gone from this world. Blumenfield knew that it was the Angel of Death peering through the knotholes of their eyes, beckoning him to the Other Side.

But Blumenfield persisted, stubbornly, the only way he knew.

The last player Blumenfield signed, a slick-fielding, college-level second baseman, had initially refused to join the team, saying that Zionism was destined for the trash bin of history like all the other nineteenth-century isms before it. Judaism was nothing more than crass tribalism, and Israel itself was an unredeemable desert wasteland. *Blumenfield found himself sprawled on the kitchen floor of his childhood home, pounding the linoleum with his knuckles, screaming bloody murder, for what? A chocolate chip cookie. He wanted that cookie so badly that he knew he would die if he did not have it. His mother, an impenetrable giant, ankles indifferent, toe tapping impatiently on the cool floor, denied his demand again.*

"But, Mumma," he cried. "I want it."

"You'll spoil your appetite for dinner."

"No cookie, no dinner," he said.

"But, you're so thin," his mother said, bending low with concern.

"Then give me the cookie."

"Remarkable," Josh said, patting Blumenfield on the shoulder. "I've never seen such hard-nosed negotiating in my life. You practically had that second baseman shining your shoes. We're done." He smiled with satisfaction. "You've got your team. Next stop, *Eretz* Israel."

"Goddammit," Blumenfield said, distractedly. "Where's my cookie, you ignorant fuck?"

The stewardess must have put something in Blumenfield's tea, because he felt himself sinking into his seat, drawn into the deep embrace of the cushioned fabric. Out the airplane's window, white clouds flew past. He heard a baby cry from somewhere behind him and he knew it was one of his own children. His vision was clouded by the glary, haloed procession of stewardesses rumbling past with their shining carts offering chop suey and rattlesnake. He knew these words, sounded them out as a bright bubble on his lips, but they meant nothing to him. Had he torn down chop suey to build rattlesnake? Had he evicted Chinamen for the sake of a snake? The words stirred up dust in his head and he tried to find his way, but that persistent undulating fist in his chest quivered like a dollar bill caught on a breeze, and then floated away.

His barber had cut his hair too short and light was coming in the top of his head; he had to close his eyes.

The stadium was full and full of light. Everyone he knew was there in the crowd, cheering. He recognized faces he had not seen in years, and faces he had forgotten: Menachem Begin was there and Greenberg, and Mayor Lindsay. Judah P. Benjamin was sitting down by the festive bunting squirting mustard onto a hot dog; and Marilyn was there, too, in the front row, every bit the vision she was before she had put on all that weight, her almond face smiling at him. And now, Blumenfield saw his old friend Moses, standing in the middle of the diamond, waving him down to the mound to throw out the first pitch of the rest of his life.

ACKNOWLEDGMENTS

I would like to thank Michael Callaghan, Lisa Foad, David Sobelman and everyone at Exile Editions for helping bring this book to life. I would also like to thank Dara Horn, Michael Wex, Steve Almond, Gary Alpert, Stephanie Goldenhersh, Rusty Barnes, Sara Blazic, Sandy Jimenez, Moosecat, and of course, Eve Rubinstein Papernick, who reads everything first and tells me what is horrible.

Earlier versions of stories from this collection have appeared in the following publications: "My Darling Sweetheart Baby" and "Skin for Skin" in *Night Train Magazine*; "What Is It Then, Between Us?" in *Nerve*; "The Last Five-Year Plan" in *Confrontation*; "There Is No Other" in *Exile: The Literary Quarterly*; "The Engines of Sodom" in *Zeek: A Jewish Journal of Thought and Culture*.